I0651682

Elizabeth Savile

Drifted together

Vol. I

Elizabeth Savile

Drifted together
Vol. I

ISBN/EAN: 9783337049614

Printed in Europe, USA, Canada, Australia, Japan

Cover: Foto ©Andreas Hilbeck / pixelio.de

More available books at **www.hansebooks.com**

DRIFTED TOGETHER.

A Novel.

BY

ELIZABETH SAVILE.

IN THREE VOLUMES.
VOL. I.

London:
SAMUEL TINSLEY & CO.,
31, SOUTHAMPTON STREET, STRAND.
1879.

To

L———.

CONTENTS OF VOL. I.

DRIFTED TOGETHER.

CHAPTER I.

SHE'S WOOED AND SHE'S WON.

'VALLA, what do you think?—Winifred de Valines is going to be married!' So said a girl about twenty, as she came into the pretty morning-room where her sister was sitting.

'Winifred going to be married! Tessie, you can't mean it! Who is she going to marry?'

'You'll never guess, so I'll be merciful and tell you at once—Lord Mortimer.'

'Lord Mortimer! Nonsense! it's impossible, he's so old, and besides, he's not the least like a marrying man! Who has told you such a thing?'

'Papa; he heard it this morning from Uncle Hugh, who says it is not only perfectly true, but that they are to be married in a few weeks.'

'Well, I never should have imagined such a thing. Fancy little Winnie being Lady Mortimer! What shall we give her, Tessie? we must get her a present.'

'Yes, certainly;' and then the two sisters went on to talk over some other bits of news, besides the intelligence which had so interested them.

Valentina and Theresa Lynton were twin sisters, daughters of Lord Elmarch; their mother had been dead for many years, and they had only one brother in the army.

Winifred de Valines was about a year younger than they were, and during the past season they had become great friends. Valla and Tessie also knew Lord Mortimer slightly, but neither of them had ever regarded him as a man likely to marry a girl so many years younger than himself. And truly, many others were surprised at the announcement of the engagement beside the Lyntons. Rupert, ninth Earl of Mortimer, was verging on forty: he was grave, and rather stern in appearance, but one of the best and kindest men in existence. He was rich, too, and his place, Mortimer Castle, was a lovely one.

Why had he never married? That was a question many people had asked, and though various reasons were conjectured, no one had divined the simple truth—that he had never taken a fancy to any of the numerous fair

maidens who were ready to become Lady
Mortimer ; never, that is to say, till he saw
Winifred de Valines, and then the grave earl
fell desperately in love with the bright little
girl of nineteen. She began by regarding
him with the greatest admiration, and soon
came to like him better than any of her
younger admirers. So one bright morning,
early in September, when both were staying
at the house of her uncle, Lord Aston, he
asked her to be his wife, she said ' Yes,' and
gave the whole of her young heart to him
whom she thought the first of men. Her
father and mother were perhaps somewhat
surprised at her choice, but no objections
could be made, and the marriage was to take
place at the end of October.

Colonel and Lady Mary de Valines had
five children ; the eldest, Geoffrey, was
twenty-two, and in the Guards ; Winnie

came next, she was past nineteen; then Katharine, more generally known as Kitty, who was eighteen; after her Charlie, an Eton boy; and the youngest was Mabel, who was eleven. Kitty was a very pretty girl, with blue eyes and fair hair, much taller than her eldest sister, who was on a small scale, with tiny hands and feet, dark brown hair and eyes, and a very expressive face. No wonder Winnie had fascinated Lord Mortimer, for she was one of the brightest little creatures in the world, and clever as well.

Lord Mortimer had no brothers or sisters; indeed, his nearest relations were cousins, and he had not many of them; but of the few, there was one by whom his marriage might be disliked in proportion to the disappointment it must occasion. This was Tom Percival, heir-presumptive to the Mor-

timer title, and friend as well as relation
to its present possessor. But, fortunately,
Tom was far too good-natured and easy-
going an individual to trouble himself with
thoughts of his own interest; he was surprised, like the rest of the world, but no one
gave heartier congratulations, and from no
one did Lord Mortimer value them more.

'I say, old fellow, I wish you joy! you
must introduce me to my cousin-elect.' This
was the greeting of the disappointed heir,
when next he met Lord Mortimer, after the
announcement of his engagement.

'Thank you, Tom; indeed, I want you to
know her. Come with me now, will you,
and make her acquaintance? She, with her
father and mother, came up to Eaton Square
yesterday.'

'Willingly,' and the two started off together. October was just beginning, and, as

the marriage was to be on the twenty-eighth, Winnie and her parents had come up to London for some of the multifarious business a wedding always entails, not the least important, certainly, being the selection of a trousseau.

Winifred was looking her best that morning, as she sat in the pretty drawing-room writing a letter, dressed in soft grey, and with a splendid diamond engagement-ring sparkling on the third finger of her left hand. She raised her eyes as the door opened, and a gleam of pleasure lit up her face as she came forward to welcome the earl.

'Winnie, I have brought my cousin, Tom Percival, to introduce to you,' he said, as he greeted her.

With a half shy but very attractive manner she put out her hand, and Tom was charmed at her soft voice and graceful movements, and when they sat down and Lord Mortimer began to talk to her, he found plenty of opportunity to take a good view of her.

'She's a nice little thing,' was his mental comment—'good-looking, but not so pretty as I expected; she does look very young, but Mortimer will take very good care of her, and I never saw a man look happier than he does.'

And certainly his lordship did look happy as he talked to his betrothed. People called him cold and stern, but Tom Percival knew him better, and was aware of what a depth of feeling and warmth of heart he really possessed, and his devotion to Winnie was no ordinary one, but stronger than even she was aware of. The two cousins had not been very long in Eaton

Square, when Lady Mary came in. She was a quiet gentle person, not the least like her daughter, but very pleasant, and easy to get on with, as Tom Percival soon found; for, as may be supposed, he was left for her to entertain. At last he rose, rejecting all offers of luncheon, as he had an engagement, and walked off well pleased with his introduction to the future Lady Mortimer.

'So that is your cousin, Rupert?' said Winnie, when he was gone; 'he seems very pleasant; he's a barrister, isn't he?'

'Yes, he is a capital fellow, so good-natured, and yet thoroughly high-principled. He's about eight-and-twenty, though he does not look it.'

'No,' said Lady Mary, 'I took him for about two or three and twenty; but he is so fair and boyish-looking, that one would never guess his real age.'

'Oh !' as Colonel de Valines came in ; 'you've just missed Mr. Percival, Henry. I am sorry you did not see him.'

'Yes,' replied her husband, 'I would have come in sooner had I known he was here. There, Winnie,' as he handed her a parcel, 'that's for you. I met Lord Elmarch just now, and he said he was on his way to leave it here ; but as he's only in London for two days he was rather glad, I think, to be relieved of it.'

'Oh, thank you, papa,' said Winnie, as she rapidly unfolded the wrappings and disclosed to view a very pretty fan ; 'it's from Valla and Tessie.'

The fan was duly admired, and then Lord Mortimer said :

'The Miss Lynton you call Tessie is the youngest of the two sisters, isn't she ?'

'Yes, she is ; but they are twins, and so the difference is very small : they are great friends of mine, especially Valla.   You know them, don't you, Rupert ?'

'A little,' was his answer, and then an interruption came; and in the afternoon Lord Mortimer took Winnie out riding in the deserted ' Row.'

The name of Tessie Lynton had recalled to Lord Mortimer's recollection a story of nearly two years previous respecting her probable marriage to one of his country neighbours, the son of Sir Hugh Royle, of Royle Abbey.   But the engagement, if there had been one—and of this Lord Mortimer was not sure—had been broken off in consequence of Lord Elmarch's discovering how thoroughly good-for-nothing was the man who had won poor Tessie's affections.   She had never combated her father's decision,

but deep in her heart there still lurked a
secret liking for John Royle, who, worthless
as he was, was a very fascinating man. How
worthless, few knew better than Lord Mortimer, through his long friendship with the
Royle family.

Colonel de Valines's place was only about
thirty miles south of London, and the wedding was to take place from thence ; he had
inherited a large fortune from his mother,
the only daughter of a wealthy country squire.
The old squire had adored his only daughter,
and when she set her heart on marrying a
penniless younger son of Lord Carmouth,
he bought Skeatings for her home, as his
own estate descended to male heirs.

Mrs. de Valines had been dead for some
years, and her eldest son had succeeded her.
Lady Mary was a sister of Lord Aston's
and a distant cousin of her husband's.

The home at Skeatings had been a very happy one, and Winnie's approaching marriage would make a sad break in the hitherto united circle ; but her prospects were so bright, and she was so happy in them, that her parents could not regret her loss, though it would deprive them of one of their darlings. And even Winnie thought with sorrow of leaving her home, and all the dear ones in it ; she was most thoroughly in love with Lord Mortimer, but she was also a very affectionate daughter and sister, and she could not help feeling regret at leaving her childhood's home.

But the day came at last, and was as bright a one as any young bride could desire—like a summer's day that had dropped into October by mistake.

All went off well, and the wedding was very much like other weddings, while no

happy pair ever began their married life
more prosperously and happily than Lord
and Lady Mortimer.

CHAPTER II.

ROYLE ABBEY.

'How shall frayle pen describe her heavenly face,
For feare, through want of skill, her beauty to disgrace.'
FAERIE QUEENE.

'Is Miss Royle at home?' asked an elderly lady in a pony-carriage, as the servant opened the door at Royle Abbey, two days after Lord Mortimer's marriage.

'Yes, ma'am.'

And throwing her reins to the groom, she entered the low, dark entrance-hall, and following the servant as he opened a door on the left and announced 'Miss Haleswell,' found herself in the library.

It was a comfortable room, panelled with dark oak, and with well-stocked bookshelves, and a Turkey carpet.

The windows, the most modern-looking part of the room, opened on to a terrace, and looked over a pleasant sweep of park, with hills in the distance.

On a couch by the fireside lay a slight, pale figure, with the fragile appearance of a confirmed invalid. This was Cicely Royle, the second daughter of Sir Hugh Royle, the present possessor of Royle. His family consisted of one son and three daughters, the only survivors of nine children; his wife having died many years before the time of which we are speaking.

A dark cloud of trouble and sorrow had descended on the Royles of Royle Abbey, and it seemed as if they really were an ill-fated race. One son, a bright-eyed midship-man, had gone down with his ship one stormy night soon after his mother's death, while the eldest, Alan Royle, with his young wife and child, had been among the victims of the Indian Mutiny. Two little girls had been carried off by scarlet-fever, and another had died in infancy.

Of the four who remained, John Royle was heartless, extravagant and unprincipled, and it was not wonderful that Lord Elmarch had refused to allow his daughter to engage herself to such a man. Cicely was confined to the sofa in consequence of a bad fall; and Lilian, the youngest, was not quite eighteen.

Lilian Royle was a beauty in every sense of the word. Her figure was tall and grace-ful, her features perfectly formed, her com-

plexion was clear and pale, and all this, combined with large dark eyes and dark auburn
hair, formed a *tout ensemble* which was really
enchanting. She was a bright, happy creature, devoted to hunting or any kind of
active amusements, was the light of the
whole house and the darling of her father's
and sisters' hearts

But the Royles were all handsome, both
men and women; the pictures in the long
gallery of the Abbey, the Vandycks, the
Lelys, the Sir Joshuas, and the Gains-
boroughs, all told the same tale of loveli-
ness; and the only plain one in the family
was Mary Royle, the eldest daughter. Poor
Mary! hers was a hard life; she was the
mainstay of all, and struggled bravely to
keep things going; for somehow the estate
did not bring in so much as formerly, and
John Royle's extravagance had compelled Sir

Hugh to mortgage the property as heavily as he dared.

Sir Hugh himself was a thorough English country gentleman, kind-hearted, and open-handed; not very wise or clever, but a popular man and an affectionate father.

As Miss Haleswell entered the library, Mary Royle rose from a low chair by the side of her sister's couch, and came forward to greet her. After the old lady had made particular inquiries about Cicely's health, she sat down in a large arm-chair, and began to talk about the great event of the neighbourhood—Lord Mortimer's marriage.

Now, report had whispered that Mary Royle had been in love with Lord Mortimer, and Miss Haleswell was well aware of this; but she knew that it was of no use to avoid the subject, as Mary would have to hear his marriage perpetually discussed, and that the best way was to ignore bygones.

'I see that Lord Mortimer's marriage is duly announced in the *Times*,' said Miss Haleswell, 'not to mention a long account of it in the *Morning Post*. What a lovely day they had for it! I have been hearing a great deal of the bride from my cousin Cecil Vernon, who knows the De Valines very well.'

'Oh, do tell us what he said of her,' said Mary; 'we are so anxious to know if she is likely to prove a pleasant neighbour.'

And Miss Haleswell noticed with satisfaction that she spoke with perfect nonchalance.

'Well, this is what Cecil said when I asked him if she was pretty : "No, not pretty, nice-looking enough, a very bright merry girl, but rather too small ; her sister, who has not been out long, is much **better looking,** and the jolliest **girl** in the world." Whereupon, as you may suppose, I began to chaff Cis about the young lady, and **though he laughed it off,** I suspect he is rather smitten, though I don't suppose it is serious. **However,** he further told me that the **De Valines** are charming people, **and that** he considered Lord Mortimer a very lucky man to have got such a nice wife, and that we shall find her a great acquisition in the neighbourhood. So this sounds **very** pleasant.'

'Indeed it does. I hear that Lord and Lady Mortimer are coming to the **Castle** in ten days.'

'Yes, so Mr. Stapleton told me; and I hope that we shall **have some** gaiety during the winter, which will **be very nice for Lilian. How is she ?'**

'Oh, very well; she is out hunting with

my father. The hounds met at Manby this morning, and they hoped to have a good run.'

' She seems fonder than ever of hunting, and I hear she rides splendidly ; she is growing lovelier than ever, Mary.'

' I think she is ; but I am always afraid we rate her too highly, and that other people will not admire her so much.'

' They can't help themselves : she is—but there, I can't say what she is, excepting that in my eyes she is perfection.'

' Ah, Miss Haleswell,' said Cicely, smiling, ' I'm afraid you are too partial a judge : you always spoil her ; indeed you spoil everybody.'

' I—no indeed, my dear,' said Miss Haleswell. ' I'm a great deal too sharp-sighted for that,' and she laughed merrily. ' By the way, Cicely, how is your embroidery getting on ? for I have brought you a fresh order.'

' I have almost finished the handkerchiefs,' said Cicely, displaying her work, for her chief occupation was in embroidery in all kinds of materials, which she disposed of for charities, and Miss Haleswell frequently brought her orders, having a large number of friends and acquaintances, who were glad to obtain the beautiful work which Cicely Royle's skilful fingers executed.

Miss Haleswell, elderly heiress as she was, or rather now possessor of a large fortune, had had much of romance in her life ; and though she had never married, rumour credited her with having had forty proposals. When she was one and twenty she had in-herited from her uncle an estate, and nine thousand a year. Her father had died when she was a child, and when the property came into her own power, she had gone with her mother to live at Elm Court, the name of her new home. She was then a merry good-tempered girl, tall and slight, with a bright colour and yellowish hair; not good-looking, but very popular, even without her money. With it, of course, she was everywhere *fêted*, flattered, and made love to.

But Emma Haleswell was not deceived; she knew that she owed all this attention to her riches, and she remained perfectly heart-whole, till one day a young officer was introduced to her, who soon succeeded in winning her affections. He was not rich, but had a sufficient income, and all seemed bright before them; but some slight difference arose, and slanderous tongues made mischief between Miss Haleswell and her lover. While on the one hand they made Miss Haleswell believe she was sought only for her money, **on the** other, they taunted her *fiancé* with his cleverness in securing the heiress. **A** breach was effected, **and, '** Alas, how easily things go wrong !' 'life was never the same **again ' for** either of them.

The officer **had married and died, and** Miss Haleswell, after finding things **very** blank **and** dreary **for a year** or two, had **summoned her** resolution, **and** bravely faced **the** future, resolving **that** she would be **an old** maid ; and she never changed her mind, though she had many temptations to do so.

She would often laugh over **the** recollections of her numerous admirers, and **now** that years had softened the memory of her lost love, she was **as** happy an old maid as you could find. She was also the kindest-hearted creature imaginable, and her charities, known and unknown, were boundless.

People wondered who would be her heir, as her property was entirely in her own power, and many thought that handsome Cecil Vernon, of the Hussars, her distant cousin, had a good chance of succeeding her. Others said that her dearest friends, the Royles, were likely to profit by her fortune, and in her secret heart the old lady cherished a hope that Cis Vernon would take a fancy to Lilian Royle, in which case, she intended to acknowledge him at once as her heir.

So, though she had chaffed Cis about Kitty de Valines, she was hoping that he and her favourite Lilian might be brought together. For Miss Haleswell felt deeply for the many sorrows of the Royles, and dreaded lest the fair face of Lilian should bring her any of the suffering which seemed inseparable from her name; and in her scheme for the marriage of Lilian with

Cecil, she hoped to secure for her a happy future, an exemption from the ruin which sooner or later she feared that John Royle's extravagance would bring on his family.

CHAPTER III.

FESTIVITIES.

'Tell me all about Muddlesham Hall ;
  Say who were the favourites there,
And who shone as the belle of the ball.'

KNAPP.

MORTIMER CASTLE stood in the midst of some
of the loveliest scenery in X-shire. The park
which surrounded it was of some miles'
extent, but one of its lodges led into the
little village of Combe Mortimer, which
was only about a mile from the Castle.

Combe was a pretty little place, with an
old-fashioned air about its picturesque cot-

tages, grouped round the large green, on one side of which stood the beautiful lately-restored church, close by a snug rectory, and near to the rectory some model village schools.

Combe was an old-fashioned village, too, in other respects. The owners of Mortimer Castle had not only possessed the privileges, but had performed the duties of 'lords of the soil,' and so were looked up to, and indeed adored by their poorer neighbours; for there is still some old feudal feeling left in England, and where the landlords have fulfilled their duties rightly, they may generally find appreciation and affection from their tenants and labourers, who look on the owner of the great house of the place as some one reflecting glory on them, some one of whom they have a right to be proud.

At any rate Lord Mortimer was so regarded by the inhabitants of Combe, and

from old Betty Mullins in the almshouses, up
to Thomas Katt, the well-to-do shopkeeper ;
from Mr. Stephenson, the rector, down to
the smallest school-child, there was not one
who had not taken the keenest interest in 'my
lord's marriage,' or who had not wished him all
possible prosperity from the bottom of their
hearts.

So when Lord and Lady Mortimer came
home about the middle of November, they
met with an enthusiastic reception ; and if the
curiosity which was felt to see the young bride
was hardly satisfied when the Combe Mortimer people found she was too small and slight
for their ideas of a countess, yet they were
consoled by her bright smiles and sweet expression, and also by the unmistakable happiness visible on the faces of both bride and
bridegroom. And when in the course of a
few weeks they made her acquaintance, as

she went about amongst the cottages, their hearts were quite won, and they pronounced as their verdict, that she was worthy of her husband.

Very happy were those first few weeks of married life to both husband and wife. Winifred had so much to see and to hear; and Lord Mortimer was by no means an idle man, but one who not only took his full share in county business, but really filled his place in the House of Lords, and was always active in all measures of improvement and benevolence.

Into all his plans and occupations his wife entered with the keenest interest; she was sufficiently clever to take pleasure in them, and delighted also to find an outlet for some of her schemes of doing good to others by helping her husband in his varied business.

It was arranged that at the beginning of
January a large party should assemble at
the Castle, and a ball and other festivities
be given to inaugurate the reign of the new
Lady Mortimer; and at last the day arrived,
and Mortimer Castle was filled to overflow-
ing. There were to be some *tableaux* on
Monday evening, and one of the sitting-
rooms had been prettily arranged as a
theatre; then on Tuesday the ball was to
take place; while on Thursday there was
also a ball at Cheston, the neighbouring
town. There was to be dancing on the unoccupied nights, and a meet of the X-shire
hounds on Saturday morning, and shooting
in Lord Mortimer's well-stocked preserves
all through the week.

So there was a fair programme of amusement for the expected guests, who when
they were assembled formed a large party.

Lilian looking more beautiful than ever in her white dress. Geoffrey was on the watch for her, and cleverly intercepting one or two other partners, carried her off to join the dancers.

Meanwhile Kitty and her partner were in animated conversation.

'Where is your regiment going when you leave X—— ?' she was asking.

'To India, I am sorry to say,' he replied.

'To India!' and Cis Vernon was well pleased to detect a faint shade of regret in her voice. 'Oh, but you will like that, won't you? You will shoot tigers instead of pheasants, and ride elephants instead of hunters, and—oh, but people are always doing something amusing in India.'

'I am not so sure about that; and then think of the heat, and the snakes, and the banishment from civilised life—at least, from

European life, which is the only kind of
civilisation I care for.'

'Well, I think India must be rather a
pleasant place altogether, and at least it will
be a complete change. I always had rather
a fancy to go to India.'

'India would be a very different place to
me if you—if all the present company were
going there,' was his rather confused answer.
'As it is, I often find it in my heart to wish
that her Majesty's dominions did not include
the Indian Empire. There, can you forgive
such an unpatriotic sentiment? and come and
have some tea.'

Geoffrey de Valines, meanwhile, oblivious
of his sister's hopes with regard to Valla
Lynton, was fast becoming desperately in
love with Lilian Royle.

She was too simple and fresh in ball-room
ways to think anything of the number of

dances in which they were partners, and she regarded him only as a capital dancer, and as very amusing to talk to ; but her verdict of the ball was enthusiastic. Never had there been anything so delightful : she wished she could go to a ball every night ; only, why did it ever come to an end ? What a contrast was her bright beauty to the plain, worn face of her eldest sister !

Mary Royle had but few partners, but her friends were many ; and though she had long ceased to look on balls as scenes of enchantment, she found this one a very pleasant change from the monotony of her daily life, and treasured up every detail respecting the entertainment to amuse Cicely with, on her return ; while she felt 'an elder sister's pride' in listening to the universal admiration of her darling Lilian.

Mary Royle had quite overcome her

girlish devotion to Lord Mortimer ; indeed, it
had not been a very deep feeling, and home
cares and anxieties had engrossed her so
much as almost to make her forget that she
had ever cared for him ; and she could see
his entire affection for his bright young wife
without the least pain, and felt a sort of
amused wonder when she remembered that
she had once contemplated the idea of becoming mistress of Mortimer Castle ; and as
she watched her young hostess in her indefatigable efforts to entertain her guests, she
said to herself :

'It is much better as it is ; I was never
fitted for the position, and could not have
filled it properly.'

So the ball came to an end at last ; after
all, it was exactly like other balls, and people
made the usual hackneyed remarks on the
beauty of the flowers and the excellence of

the lighting, and agreed that it **was** a perfect **floor.**

The country neighbours congratulated each **other also on what** they hoped was a **commencement** of a long series **of** festivities at Mortimer, **and expressed** their approval **of its owner's marriage.**

Winnie enjoyed it immensely : she did not however dance rounds, as Lord Mortimer had a particular objection **to** his wife's valsing ; and **though with** some regret, she **was** too devoted a wife **not** to acquiesce in his prohibition. She was not sorry when once or twice in the evening, her husband came **up** and said : ' Winnie, come and have a turn ;' **for** he was **a** really **good** dancer, and their steps suited perfectly. **Indeed, as** they floated round the room together **to** the strains **of** the last new valse, played with **great spirit** by Coote **and** Tinney's band,

Sir Hugh Royle said to his neighbour,
Lady Ashby :

'That's what I call dancing. Reminds
me of my young days, when I was as fond of
balls as any one ; but most of the people
now don't dance, they only jump about—
there !' as an energetic couple charged him
with all their strength, and very nearly
knocked him over ; ' did you ever see anything like it ? People who can't dance ought
to be forbidden to attempt it by Act of
Parliament. There, Mynors, you might
bring in a Bill about it,' laughing heartily
at his own idea.

The young M.P. would have been willing
to bring in any bill that would have ensured
his dancing with Lilian Royle, but that
young lady had so many partners that she
had no dances to bestow on him ; and as he
was on the look-out for a wife, this was

rather an annoyance to Mr. Mynors, who was beginning to think that Lilian would prove well suited to reflect glory on his own taste, and was debating as to whether he should ask her to be his wife.

The idea of her refusing him never entered his head.

CHAPTER IV.

DAME CICELY'S PICTURE.

' All thoughts, all passions, all delights,
    Whatever stirs this mortal frame,
All are but ministers of Love,
    And feed his sacred flame.'

                        COLERIDGE.

Enter the house—prithee, forget it not—
And look a while upon a picture there.
'Tis of a lady in her earliest youth !'

                        ROGERS.

THE next day, when Lord Mortimer came to
his wife's boudoir, before dressing-time, for a
little chat, he found her meditating by the
fire.

'Well, Winnie, are you very tired? I think people enjoyed themselves very much last night.'

'Oh, I am not much tired really, and so glad the ball was a success. How lovely Lilian Royle is ! she was quite the beauty of the evening.'

'I think she was ; she has grown into a very striking girl. She is rather wild, though, and always does exactly as she likes ; and her father lets her hunt as often as he does himself, which is not very good for her. By the way, I think your brother Geoffrey is rather smitten with her. I hope it is not serious, for I do not think it would be a desirable connection for him in many ways, more especially as John Royle, the son, is a thorough-going scamp. I don't know any one for whom I have a greater contempt.'

'Of course, Rupert, Geoffrey would admire Lilian, but you may be quite sure his doing so is not serious, for he is a great flirt; however, I hope very much that he will marry some one quite different. I know whom I should like for a sister-in-law.'

'Brothers very seldom marry the girls their sisters select for them, Winnie; but I am glad you think it is only flirtation— there was plenty of that last night. Trent and Vernon were vying with each other in attentions to Kitty, and I think she seemed to prefer Vernon.'

'I suppose he is the best dancer; but I think the Duke of Trent really likes Kitty very much, and I hope something may come of it, for it would be such a nice marriage. As for Captain Vernon, he had better secure Miss Ashby, who will have £12,000 a year, and I am sure she likes him.'

'My dear child, I must beg you won't take to match-making, it is a very dangerous game, and any one who embarks in it is most likely to get into a hobble. Besides, match-makers don't consider mutual likings—witness your comments on my observations—but only suitable arrangements. No, Winnie, I consider match-makers decidedly objectionable, and don't want you to become one; we did not need anything of that sort to bring us together.'

'No, of course not; but exceptions only prove the rule, so your lordship is out there,' she said, laughing. 'But it is very complimentary to you that I should be so satisfied with marriage as to wish others to embark in it; and really I don't see any harm in helping the right people to meet, and then the mutual likings may come.'

'The difficulty is as to the right people,

and I don't think a looker-on can always
judge there. However, whether there is harm
or not, I don't wish you to try your hand
at it. Are we to have a lottery again to-
night? I am sure I hope so, for then I
should have a chance of escaping her Grace
of Newport. She is really intolerable. What
do you think of her advising me last
night at supper to reduce my establishment,
especially the stable part of it, as she considered keeping so many horses led young
men into mischief? in fact, she infinitely
preferred job horses. I am not so very
young as all that, but I thanked her with
due gravity, and inquired if she also preferred hired horses to driving in her friends'
carriages. This pulled her up a little, for
she is horribly stingy, and can't bear having
to pay for flys from stations ; so she began
explaining away her own words, as she gene-

Amongst them were Colonel and Lady Mary de Valines with Geoffrey and Kitty; Lord Elmarch and his two daughters; the stiff and not very popular Duchess of Newport and her daughter Lady Jane Flavigny; Sir Charles and Lady Ashby, and their only daughter, heiress to many broad acres; Mr. and Mrs. Beauchamp; Tom Percival; the Duke of Trent, a young man of five-and-twenty, with fabulous riches, and half a dozen country houses; his great friend, Captain Cecil Vernon, who was good-looking and penniless, and cousin, as has been said, to Miss Haleswell. Besides, there was Mr. Mynors of Mynors, an M.P., very confident in his own powers, and anticipating ministerial honours in rapid succession; Teddy Guildford, reputed the best dancer in London, and a few others whom it is needless to name.

Most of the people knew each other, and promised to shake well together, an important item for the hostess, especially when she is a young one, and new to the *rôle*.

The dinner-party on Monday night included the Royles—Sir Hugh, Mary, and Lilian, who was just making her *début*. As she came into the room her wonderful beauty and tall graceful figure attracted general attention, and Geoffrey de Valines was not sorry when he found himself deputed to take her in to dinner.

' You live near here, don't you ?' he asked, as a preliminary to conversation.

' Oh yes, only five miles off,' was her reply. ' Do you know these parts ? as the old women say.'

' Not at all.   It seems a very jolly place, and capital hunting country, isn't it ?'

' Oh, perfect !' was her answer, in so en-

thusiastic a tone that his next question
was—

'Do you hunt ?'

'Three days a week, whenever the hounds
meet near enough, and I wish it could be
every day. I think hunting is the most
delicious thing in the world ; don't you ?'

'I'm very fond of it, certainly ; but do you
like it better than dancing ?'

'Much better ; though I like dancing immensely, too. But the ball here to-morrow
is to be my first real one, you know, so perhaps it will make me change my mind.'

There was something so wonderfully fresh
and unsophisticated about Lilian Royle, that
Geoffrey felt irresistibly attracted towards
her, and he congratulated himself on being
next the prettiest and liveliest girl in the
room. They kept up a merry conversation
during the remainder of dinner, and had

become great friends when the time came for the ladies to move.

Meantime Kitty's neighbour, Teddy Guildford, was doing his best to extract a full description of the coming *tableaux*, which she declared he must wait for till the proper time came.

'Now,' said he, ' I could arrange a splendid one for you : the Duchess of Newport for Queen Elizabeth, Vernon for Essex, and all you fair ladies for the maids of honour; it would be great sport. The ring scene, you know. Her Grace does not love Vernon, so I am sure she would look suitably severe as she bestows the ring and the caution. Now, confess she looks equal to keeping any number of people in order ; see how she's lecturing Lord Mortimer.'

' Oh, hush, pray. Lady Jane is quite near us ; she will certainly hear you.'

'Poor Lady Jane!' pursued he unrelentingly, though in a lower tone; 'what shall we make her? Why, Penelope unravelling her web; it will just suit her, she is such an indefatigable worker. I am sure I have met her roll of work everywhere for the last ten years; she is always stitching at it, so she must undo it at night, for it is not nearly finished; indeed I am tired of asking her when it will be done. There,' as Winifred rose, 'don't forget my valuable suggestions.'

And Kitty found it difficult not to laugh when she saw Lady Jane fly to her beloved work as soon as possible after dinner. But she had not time to stay and inquire into its progress, for it was time to go and array herself for the *tableaux*.

When the audience was ready the curtain drew up and disclosed the first *tableau :*

'LANCELOT MEETING ELAINE IN HER FATHER'S
HALL.'

It was not very difficult to recognise in the
'lily maid of Astolat' the fair skin and golden
hair of Kitty de Valines, but Geoffrey was
completely transformed as Sir Lancelot, and
the other figures were equally well got up.
The scenery and arrangements were most
carefully carried out, and the lighting, no
unimportant part, beautifully managed. The
effect had been carefully studied, and the
tableau was much admired.

Next in succession came two *tableaux* from
'The Corsair': the first—

'GULNARE VISITING CONRAD IN PRISON,'

with Lady Mortimer as Gulnare, and her
husband as Conrad.

Winnie was a capital actress, and her

whole *pose* and expression were exactly what Gulnare's might have been. It had not been easy to induce Lord Mortimer to represent Conrad, and he had exclaimed, when his wife informed him that the part would suit him perfectly, ' that he was afraid she must consider he possessed the " thousand crimes " of the Corsair, and hoped he was to be allowed the " one virtue " also owned by Conrad;' to which she had retorted, ' he would show the one virtue by consenting to take his part ;' and he had submitted, and looked as melancholy and fierce as his part required.

Then followed—

' CONRAD RETURNING TO FIND MEDORA DEAD,'

where Kitty represented Medora.

Both of these *tableaux* were thoroughly successful ; but the next one, representing

'THE COURT OF MARY STUART'

at the time of her marriage to Darnley, was the greatest success of the evening.

The beautiful and unfortunate queen was represented by Lilian Royle ; and as her intended appearance in the character had been carefully kept secret, the fair vision was totally unexpected. In truth Lilian was really an ideal Mary Stuart, and the exquisite dress suited her to perfection; while her four Maries, Darnley, Murray, and all the other celebrities of the court, were dressed in perfect accordance with the costume of the day. This *tableau* met with great applause, and was repeated in answer to the combined entreaties of the spectators.

No pains had been spared by Lady Mortimer to arrange the *tableaux*, and the perfection to which they were carried fully rewarded her efforts. Certainly, as she said herself, it was a great help to have such a representative for Queen Mary as Lilian Royle; and always enthusiastic, she was especially so now in her admiration of the girl's extreme beauty.

After the *tableaux* were over, performers and spectators alike adjourned to the ball-room to see, as they said, what the floor was like, and proceeding further to try it practically, danced away merrily for an hour.

While the dancing was going on the young hostess busied herself in match-making projects, and thinking that she saw in one or two of her guests a disposition to like what she considered the right person for them respectively to like, anticipated no difficulty in arranging some satisfactory marriages.

For one thing, she greatly desired that
her brother Geoffrey should marry Valia
Lynton ; and then, considering his want of
fortune, that Captain Vernon, whose good
looks and fascinating manners made him a
general favourite, and who was besides
Geoffrey's great friend, should repair it by
marrying quiet little Miss Ashby, the
heiress ; and Lady Mortimer was certainly
not far wrong in thinking that, as far as Miss
Ashby's own inclinations were concerned,
Captain Vernon might be tolerably sure of
success.

As for her own pretty sister, Winnie, obser-
vant of the Duke of Trent's open admiration, had quite made up her mind that Kitty
would be the future Duchess of Trent, and
aware that Lilian Royle, with all her beauty,
was not rich, she further contemplated a match
between her and Mr. Mynors of Mynors.

It was a comprehensive scheme, certainly, and occupied her little ladyship's mind in no small degree; particularly as beyond vague hints she did not intend to communicate her arrangements to her husband for fear of his laughing at or discouraging her *châteaux en Espagne;* but she determined to do all she could towards promoting the matrimonial arrangements, and came down to breakfast the next morning full of projects for getting the right pairs together.

Breakfast was, as usual, rather a heavy meal. What a blessing it would be if it was the custom for every one to have breakfast in their own rooms, when a large party is staying in the house. It is too soon in the day for society to begin, and the chances are that everybody is rather cross, and each person has his or her head full of their own letters and affairs, and is by no means inclined to enter into general conversation. Of course there are exceptions to the rule, and it is to be feared that the greatest one is, when some member of the party can announce a really startling event, the more horrible the better.

It is wonderful how cheerful and friendly people get, directly they begin discussing horrors. The public appetite for them is greater than even for fish, kidneys, and ome-lette, hot rolls, and buttered toast, though the consumption of these latter articles is not generally despised by most people; and it is surprising what an amount persons who declare they 'eat nothing for breakfast' include in that nothing.

After breakfast the men started for shoot-ing—some to slaughter pheasants, in a *grande battue,* and two or three for rabbit-shooting.

So they were happily disposed of; and

while some of the younger ladies went out riding, Lady Mary took the chaperons a tour of the gardens and hothouses, and listened patiently to the Duchess of Newport's dissertations on floriculture. For her grace, though one of those dull stupid people who are ignorant on most subjects, and yet profess to be acquainted with all, was apt to imagine herself an authority on everything which was mentioned, and the mistakes she made were a constant source of amusement to her acquaintances, which was perhaps fortunate, as it was the only amusement she was capable of giving them, though she would have been extremely indignant if she had imagined that any one could presume to laugh at her.

Winnie, meanwhile, flitted about the house to see if all the preparations for the ball were complete; for she felt somewhat excited at the idea of her first experiment in ball-giving.

That night, when the party assembled for dinner, each man drew the name of the lady he was to take in, according to the sensible plan of effecting by a lottery an easy exchange of dinner companions; for nothing is more wearisome than to go in to dinner every night of a country-house party with the same man. Of course in some cases it may be pleasant, but, as a rule, variety is as charming in this as in other things.

Certainly Teddy Guildford looked rather glum when he found fate assigned him to the Duchess of Newport, but Captain Vernon was well pleased to take in Kitty de Valines; and though Geoffrey did draw Lady Jane, yet he talked much more to his other neighbour, Valla Lynton, to the satisfaction of Winifred, who, for herself, as she sat by Mr. Mynors, was impressed by the cleverness and good sense, though not unalloyed by a consciousness of his own abilities, of the husband whom she had obligingly selected for Lilian Royle.

After dinner, when the ladies had donned their ball-dress and the 'house party' were assembled, the *tout-ensemble* was a very pretty one. The ball-room was very large, opening at one end into the conservatory, which was brilliantly lit, and at one side a door led into a suite of rooms, which were all thrown open for the benefit of the guests. Exquisite flowers were arranged about the rooms, and the walls were hung with many good pictures; while the soft colouring of the curtains and furniture harmonised perfectly with all the art treasures, beautiful old china, and rare curiosities which were scattered about.

Winnie herself looked her best in white satin and lace, and wore the beautiful Mortimer diamonds, which had been heirlooms in the family for many years.

The Duke of Trent went to claim Kitty for the first dance, but was met with the answer :

' No, I am very sorry, but I'm engaged to Captain Vernon.'

' The next, then ?'

' I shall be very glad ;' and he retreated to find another partner, muttering to himself:

' Forestalled, and by Vernon, too ; no one has a chance against him.' For the duke admired Kitty very much, and had nearly made up his mind that she should be honoured by the offer of the coronet of Trent.

The room began to fill, and just as dancing was going to begin, the Royles came in,

rally has to do, in spite of her love of laying down the law.'

'How I wish I had heard her.'

'I am sorry to abuse my guests, but I can't help it. By-the-bye, Winnie, Tom Percival is rather taken with your friend Miss Lynton.'

'With Valla? oh, I hope not, for she is the very girl I want Geoff——'

Then, suddenly perceiving what she was saying, she stopped short.

Her husband burst out laughing: 'At it again, quite irrespective of mutual likings this time. Now take care what you are about, for I really mean it.'

And there was a touch of decision in his voice which showed that he did. But as his wife went to dress for dinner, she said to herself:

'It is very provoking that Rupert is so

set against match-making; but however, I hope some of my matches will come off in spite of him. And men never see these things rightly; I am much more likely to find out which people suit each other than he is.'

But in this case Lord Mortimer had shown the most discrimination; for Geoffrey was decidedly in love with Lilian Royle, and Kitty flirting to a great extent, to say the least, with Captain Vernon.

. But their sister's eyes being wilfully blinded, she would not see how matters stood in time to place any obstacles in their way. How much she would have given some months after to have listened to her husband's words !

On Thursday evening there was a good deal of grumbling at the idea of the Cheston Ball, for, as a rule, public balls are not appreciated by parties staying in a house where there is a good ball-room.

'It is really a shame,' said Teddy Guildford, 'to leave such a perfect floor as the one in the ball-room here, to go and dance in the Cheston town-hall, where I suppose the boards will be as rough as a ploughed field.'

'I don't think the floor will be so bad,' said Lord Mortimer ; 'at least, I have given particular directions to have it attended to. But the ball itself is certainly a great infliction ; however, I am afraid it is a necessary evil, and it gives great satisfaction to the Cheston " natives." You'll have the hardest work, Tom, in view of the coming contest.'

For Tom Percival was to stand for Cheston the next time a vacancy occurred in its representation.

Tom shrugged his shoulders. 'Dear me, I suppose I shall have to dance with all the

Cheston young ladies. I hope they are tolerable-looking ; at any rate, the mayor's daughter is an uncommonly pretty girl, so I'll console myself by a valse with her.'

' And sacrifice yourself to your politics,' laughed Winnie ; ' let us hope you'll reap the reward whenever old Bridgburn retires. I am sure I shall be delighted to make some civility calls in the good cause, and I don't suppose that kind of canvassing will be illegal for me, though of course it would be for Rupert. I'll begin popularity-hunting to-night, so as to be ready in case of any emergency.'

When the Mortimer Castle party arrived at the town-hall, they found it fairly well filled, for the inhabitants had come early in order to see the arrival of the grandees. There were several parties from the country houses near, including one from Royle

Abbey, but the majority present were towns-people.

There was the old banker Mr. Sherby, very pompous and prosy, and as proud of his old established banking connection as any nobleman of his ancestors. There was his wife, quiet and unassuming, and apparently snubbed by her husband ; there were his two daughters, dressed with great magnificence, though in painfully vivid contrasts of the brightest pink and the greenest of apple-greens ; there was his son, the *parti* of Cheston, a conceited-looking youth, who tried hard to attach himself to the county people.

Then there was the mayor, a shy, silent man, very much embarrassed at opening the ball with Lady Mortimer ; there was Mrs. Boultbee, a buxom widow of sixty, who knew everybody, from Lord Mortimer down to the doctor's assistant, and who was ready for any amount of chaff and banter.

Winnie certainly fulfilled her promise of popularity-hunting, for she made herself very charming to the 'natives,' and really enjoyed the fun of their quaint remarks, exaggerated respect, and extraordinary costumes; while they pronounced that 'the countess' was the most affable young lady, and treasured up every detail of her dress for future imitation.

One old lady, a certain Miss Quatermaine, waxing confidential, whispered to her an eager entreaty to have the Duchess of Newport pointed out, and her disappointed comment delighted Winnie.

'Well, if ever! Why, her grace is not at all a personable lady, and her dress is not to be compared to Mrs. Boultbee's—no, nor her carriage either.'

It was certainly true, for the duchess's black silk and the diamonds which fastened her head-dress were far less striking than Mrs. Boultbee's gorgeous crimson satin and heavy cameo ornaments; and, as her grace was decidedly bored, she was looking remarkably cross as she scanned each individual with her eye-glass, and certainly detracted from the opinion Miss Quatermaine had imbibed, as to the necessity of a duchess being possessed of every charm and grace under the sun.

On the whole, however, the party from Mortimer amused themselves well at Cheston. Tom Percival won golden opinions, and was declared to be 'a most genteel young man,' and there was much merriment while the dress and remarks of the townspeople were discussed.

There was only one person who certainly

did not seem very happy, and that was the Duke of Trent. When the whole party had reached home, he made some excuses of urgent business, and explained to Lord Mortimer that he must leave early the next day. His host had some suspicion of the reason of his abrupt departure, and the next day his wife confided to him the secret which he had guessed. The duke had proposed to Kitty, who had refused him.

Winnie was unreasonably angry with the wrong person. 'So stupid of him,' she said, 'to be in such a hurry ; if he had only waited a little longer, I am sure Kitty would have accepted him ; but of course she was not prepared yet.'

'I don't agree with you there ; she saw a good deal of him last season, and for the last few days his attentions have been very marked, at least to lookers-on. But I am not surprised that she has refused him; I never imagined she had the least intention of doing anything else, and I only wonder Trent did not find out sooner that it was no use his thinking of her.'

'It is most unfortunate altogether,' said Winnie; 'I am so sorry about it.'

'Well, if he was determined to put it to the touch, and she did not care for him, it is better to have it over. I hope Trent won't take it greatly to heart, though he certainly was a good deal cast down last night.'

On Saturday the hounds met at Mortimer, and those of the guests who had not taken their departure early were assembled to see the meet. Lord Mortimer, Geoffrey, and Tom Percival turned out in pink, while the ladies were to follow as far as they could in a break, for Lord Mortimer set his face against ladies hunting.

There were, however, several who followed that day, and conspicuous among them was Lilian Royle, mounted on a beautiful chestnut horse. Soon after eleven they were off. Later on in the day, after a good run, the Royles, finding themselves close at home, decided not to go on any more, and asked Geoffrey de Valines, who had taken care to be near Lilian most of the day, to come in and pay them a visit. He gladly accepted, and while Sir Hugh stayed to give some directions to the grooms, followed Lilian into the library, where, as usual, Cicely lay on her couch.

Mary Royle rose to welcome Geoffrey, and introduce him to her sister; and then turning, said, ' I don't think you know my brother either;' and John Royle came forward, and the two men exchanged greetings.

Geoffrey had been about too much not to

have heard many things against John Royle, and he was surprised to find him such a pleasant-looking man. But the greatest villains do not always carry their characters stamped on their faces, and John Royle's powers to do evil would have been far less if his appearance had been less attractive.

Tall, and well formed, with straight, well-cut features, dark-brown hair and moustache, and clear blue eyes, with an easy deferential manner, and plenty of clever, amusing conversation, John Royle might well be described as a fascinating man ; and only a keen observer could detect, in the expression of his face and glance of his eyes, the heartless cruelty and utter worthlessness of his real character.

Cicely began to ask Geoffrey about the gaieties of the past week, and John Royle to question his sister about the run.

'You seem to have had a good run, Lilian ; how did Fury go ?'

'Oh, splendidly ! he pulls rather, but I don't mind that a bit, and he took the fence down by Chalk Lane like a bird. I prefer riding him to any horse in the stables.'

'Well, he's a very nice-looking horse certainly, but there are not many women who could ride him as you do. Have you had good sport in the shooting line, Mr. de Valines ?'

So addressed, Geoffrey turned round and entered into conversation with Lilian's brother, and they got on very well together. Then Sir Hugh came in, and the talk became general, while Geoffrey rarely took his eyes off Lilian. Naturally, his admiration did not escape the keen eyes of John Royle, and, rapidly taking in the whole situation, he decided that to encourage the flirtation might prove profitable to himself. He knew that the De Valines' property was good, and was perfectly aware that Geoffrey had the reputation of being a generous open-handed young fellow, full of life and fun, and knew also that he had a good allowance.

At this particular time John Royle was very hard up, in fact he had come down to the Abbey solely to induce his father to raise some thousands to keep his head above water; and having had rather a stormy interview with Sir Hugh after his unexpected arrival on the previous evening, when his father had told him that he could no longer continue to raise money for him, and that the present sum required must be the last one supplied, he was turning over in his head the various ways of making and winning money, with which long habit had made him almost as familiar as with the squandering of it when obtained. He was aware that Geoffrey was a member of the club he most resorted to— no other than Stacy's—where report said the play was higher than at any other club in London, and he welcomed this chance meeting as a means of making Geoffrey's acquaintance, and of inducing him to join in some of those rubbers of whist in which John Royle's luck was proverbial. So he spared no pains to make himself agreeable, and finding that Geoffrey was going up to London on the next Monday, asked him to dine with him at Stacy's on the Tuesday. Geoffrey, only too willing to become better acquainted with Lilian's brother, gladly accepted, and so fell into the trap so skillfully laid for him. When, after a long afternoon at Royle, he rode back to Mortimer, he found Winnie and her husband together in the library.

' Why, Geoffrey, where have you been ?'

said his sister. 'Rupert came home long ago.'

'Sir Hugh asked me to come in at Royle,' answered her brother, 'so I have been paying a visit there; and made acquaintance with his son, who is down for a day or two.'

'I am sorry to hear it,' was Lord Mortimer's comment; 'take care you don't get into his clutches, Geoffrey.'

'Oh, I am not afraid,' was his answer, laughing. 'I've heard enough about John Royle, but really I don't think he's quite so black as he's painted. What a fine old place the Abbey is, though!'

'Indeed it is,' said Winnie; 'and the picture gallery is beautiful. I've only just seen it, but Miss Royle asked me to go over to luncheon one day next week, that I might really explore the house.'

'They seem very pleasant people,' said Geoffrey, carelessly; 'and Miss Lilian Royle is certainly very pretty.'

'Pretty? why she's beautiful!' exclaimed his sister, quite blinded by his careless tone, and not guessing at his real sentiments. 'She rides so well, too; she was on that wonderful chestnut to-day.'

'Yes, it's a fine horse; and that's a capital one, Mortimer, you mounted me on to-day—where did you get him?'

And they began a conversation about horses, which, together with Geoffrey's well-acted indifference, completely satisfied Lord Mortimer that his brother-in-law's admiration of Lilian Royle was not serious, while his wife plumed herself on her discernment, and complacently thought how wrong Rupert had been.

Geoffrey de Valines could hardly have

explained to himself why he was so desirous that neither Lord Mortimer nor Winnie should suspect his devotion to Lilian Royle. The feeling was partly shyness, and partly, perhaps, a sort of consciousness that they might disapprove of the connection ; though this must have come to him instinctively, as he was aware that the Mortimers and Royles had been friends for generations, and was ignorant as to Lord Mortimer's views on the subject.

'Still,' said Geoffrey to himself, as he thought the matter over, 'I had rather no one suspected this ; besides, I am not in the least sure whether Lilian likes me or not yet. I've been spoony on other girls before now, and have not minded being chaffed about them, but I've never felt like this. I'm in love this time, and no mistake.'

On Monday, Geoffrey de Valines took his

departure ; and travelling up to London with
John Royle, thought more than ever that
that gentleman was painted very much
blacker than he need be.

In the afternoon, Winnie had a visit from
Miss Haleswell ; they naturally discussed
the past week's gaieties. Miss Haleswell's
home was some ten miles from Mortimer, so Winnie had only seen her at the
ball, as in previous visits they had missed
each other.

'My young cousin, Cis Vernon, enjoyed
his visit to you immensely,' said Miss
Haleswell, in the course of conversation.

'Oh; is he a cousin of yours?' asked
Winnie. 'I am so glad he was amused;
he's a great friend of my brother Geoffrey;
and we all like him so much.'

'He's not a very near relation of mine,'

remarked Miss Haleswell; 'but then I have so few connections that I am very glad to know those I have, and I am very fond of Cis. He has been my great favourite ever since he was a boy, when I lost my godson Alan Royle, who, you know, perished with his wife and their tiny baby in the Indian Mutiny.'

'So I have heard. How many troubles the Royles seem to have had!'

'Indeed, I fear that they are an ill-fated race; and when one looks at John Royle, and thinks of what he is, it is to be feared that there is more trouble in store for them yet. Alan was so different—so good and kind; his loss broke poor Lady Royle's heart, and she only lived a few months after she heard of it. And then Cicely, who was such a merry girl, got that terrible fall downstairs, and has been on her back ever since;

though now she's more cheerful than most people.'

'That she is !' responded Winnie warmly. 'I have only seen her twice, but I was very much struck with her sweet brightness.'

'I often say she's an example to us all,' said Miss Haleswell, a little huskily. 'And yet sometimes I think Mary Royle has a worse life, for she has all the burden of the whole family on her shoulders.'

'She looks very sad and careworn ; but Sir Hugh is lively enough.'

'Sir Hugh, my dear Lady Mortimer, is one of those men on whom troubles make no impression ; he has had them of every kind, but he never takes anything to heart, and, in spite of all his money-worries, and I am afraid they are pretty considerable, never gives himself a thought as to what the future may bring. I believe he would be quite happy if he had not a shilling in his pocket, and I think sometimes he'll come to that.'

Miss Haleswell knew Sir Hugh's character pretty well, and it was her own shrewd estimate of it which had led her long ago to refuse to become the mistress of Royle Abbey. Her rejection of him had not interfered with their friendship, and she had dearly loved his wife, and regarded his children as relations of her own. Still she had often congratulated herself that she had not married a man to whom no experience could teach wisdom, and whose recklessness and good-nature had done so much harm to those whom he loved the best.

How many men there are in the world like Sir Hugh Royle, on whom anxiety, trouble, grief, ay, and even disgrace, make no lasting impression; who are sunny and joyous when others would hardly be able to hold up their heads; full of fun and merriment when those who hear them can but wonder at their mood—men who, in spite of all their failings, are popular with all, and welcome everywhere, and who are missed when they pass away from our ken, far more than men of higher aims and better deeds. It is only the belongings of these individuals who are not carried away by the general verdict; it is their wives and daughters whose burdens are rendered heavier by the good-tempered nonchalance of their lords and masters.

Later on in the week, Winnie rode over to Royle Abbey, and was shown all its curiosities, and examined the picture gallery with great interest.

' Who is that ?' she asked, stopping before a picture of a grim man in an official dress.

'That,' answered Mary Royle, 'is Lord Keeper Royle—not a worthy character, I am afraid; his picture is supposed to be by Holbein.'

'Oh, what a lovely Vandyck!' and Lady Mortimer stood entranced before the picture of a young and beautiful girl, in the costume of the time.

'Yes; that,' answered her *cicerone,* 'is Dame Cicely Royle. She was very beautiful, and her story is very interesting. Cicely, her namesake, will tell you about it, if you care to hear it.'

'I should like it of all things;' and when her tour of inspection was finished, she seated herself by Cicely's couch, and petitioned for the true tale of Dame Cicely.

'Her picture quite fascinates me,' she said; 'it is so like your sister Lilian, and I am quite curious to know her history.

'It is a sad one altogether,' said Cicely; 'but what we most honour her for was her great loyalty and bravery. Her maiden name was Vandeleur; and when Vandyck painted her picture she had only been married two years, and was just nineteen. It was before the civil war began; and when it did, her husband—he was a Sir Hugh—raised a troop of horse and fought for the king.

'At Naseby he was desperately wounded, and a messenger came to summon his wife to him. About an hour before this messenger arrived, Dame Cicely had received some despatches of importance, which were to be forwarded to Prince Rupert; and having to start immediately, she thought it safer to take them with her, more especially as if the Roundheads wished to take possession of Royle, there was no possibility of any defence being made against them.

'So poor Dame Cicely left her two little boys, Alan and Hugh, to the care of a faithful old nurse and two or three old retainers, and rode off to the farm to which her husband had been taken. It was late in the day when she started, and soon became too dark to go on, while she was still some miles from her destination.

'Her guide did not know his way in the darkness; and at last, seing some lights, they stopped at a little wayside inn, and went there to rest their horses, and try and find out the direction they ought to take. But when Dame Cicely went inside, she found herself surrounded by Roundhead soldiers.

'One can fancy her horror, especially when, seeing her to be a Royalist lady, they treated her with great roughness, and pulled off her cloak and hood. Fortunately the

despatches were safely concealed in her
dress ; but whether in jest, or whether they
really suspected her of possessing any information, they declared that she was their
prisoner, and that they would take her to
the head-quarters of their general.

'Vainly she pleaded that she was only going
to see her dying husband ; vainly she im-
plored them to let a defenceless woman go
on her way. Compassion and mercy were
unknown to Cromwell's troopers, and they
paid no attention to her entreaties. Then
she grew desperate, feeling that not only
her husband was needing her, but that she
had charge of the despatches, which she
was aware contained secret news of importance. However, she was utterly
helpless, and felt that her only course was
to appear to resign herself to her fate ; so
she ceased her remonstrances, and crouched

near the fire of the rude tavern kitchen under plea of cold.

'Here she sat watching till the soldiers, tired with their march and heavy with drink, one after another fell asleep ; and then, carefully taking out the despatches, she broke the seals, and read them over, ever glancing, as she did so, at her sleeping captors, in case their slumbers might be interrupted.

'Then, bending forward, she placed the precious documents amongst the embers, and watched them consume with breathless anxiety. They were almost reduced to ashes, when some far-off sound made one of the soldiers start to his feet, and the next instant he had seized Cicely with an iron grasp.

'"So thou dost burn thy papers, woman, false malignant that thou art ! Their contents shall be forced from thy lips when our general hears this tale."

' Dame Cicely felt that any further appeal was useless ; but although the agonising sensation thrilled through her, that now she should never reach the side of her dying husband, she came to the firm determination that nothing should induce her to reveal the secrets of the burnt despatches. And bravely she kept her resolution, even when dragged before the harsh Puritan commander, who spared no threats to prevail on her to give him the information she possessed ; yes, she kept it even when he offered her an escort to her husband if she would only betray the Royalist secret, saying calmly :

' " I would not purchase the sight of my husband in his last moments by an act of dishonour ; and if I could do it, he would spurn from him a wife who had betrayed the cause which is dearer to him than life."

'So she was detained by the Roundheads for many weary months; and when, at last released, she returned to Royle Abbey, it was to find that her husband had died three days after her forcible detention. Brokenhearted widow though she was, she journeyed, in spite of all the dangers of the way, to Prince Rupert's head-quarters, and gave him, though late, the information, the possession and concealment of which had cost her so dear.

'So, Lady Mortimer, you will not wonder that we regard Dame Cicely with the greatest veneration.'

'No, indeed; thank you so much for telling me her story. It is beautiful to hear of her loyalty and devotion; but what dreadful sorrow for her to be kept from her husband when he was dying! Did she live long afterwards?'

'Yes, a good many years : she lived till after the Restoration, and the Royles were better treated by Charles II. than many other of the Cavalier families ; but her life was principally spent in doing good amongst the poor. There is still a weekly donation in bread, given away in this parish, for which she left provision in her will, and which is called " Dame Cicely's " dole.'

'Well, she is an ancestor to be proud of : you must like being named after her.'

'Yes, I do ; I am very proud of my name.'

'What stirring lives people led in those times !' said Winnie ; 'it must have been very exciting. There is not much chance in these days of doing anything remarkable.'

'Oh, I don't agree with you ; there is plenty to do—not always remarkable certainly, and that is where people make so many mistakes, by looking out for the wrong thing, and neglecting the one which is in their power to do. I am no advocate for women's rights, Lady Mortimer ; but I think every woman, especially every married .woman, has a great power in her own hands. These are not days for any one to be idle ; it is a busy age, and the only difficulty is to be busy about the right thing.'

'It is quite true ; that is a difficulty, and very often one lives in a perpetual whirl.'

'Yes, and you must have a great many of those little interruptions which always come to any one with a house and position to keep up ; but then those things are really part of your business. It is people who lead quiet lives like me who have more scope for choosing their occupations.'

Winnie looked sympathisingly at the pale

face and fragile form beside her, and thought how wonderful it was that Cicely could enter into life so thoroughly and cheerfully, debarred as she was from active participation in it ; but she only said :

'That reminds me I wanted to ask you about your training-school for girls.'

'Training-school. is almost too grand a name to give it. My father lets me have a good-sized cottage, and I have been lucky in securing a capital woman to live in it, and take charge of the four or five girls who are generally in it at a time. She teaches them how to cook, and do housemaid's work, and especially to be good laundresses ; they take in washing, which helps to support them, and a few kind friends subscribe to it. So that as the whole arrangement is very simple, and the girls live much as they would do in their own homes. I find the deficit in the receipts, which I make up by work, is not very large. Then three times a week the girls come up here, and I read a little with them, which is a great interest to me, and one or more of them comes sometimes to help in the kitchen or house here, which helps to teach them also. My great object is to make them useful servants, but not grand ones, and hitherto the results have been successful.'

'I think it is a capital arrangement, and it is so much wanted now, for everybody joins in complaining of the difficulty of getting good servants. Not that I have found any at present,' she added, laughing; 'but then with Mrs. Warner, the delightful old housekeeper at Mortimer, my task is a very easy one.'

'Yes, a really good old servant, of the old-fashioned type, is a great treasure; I am afraid the present generation will not come up to their "forbears," in respect of good service. But perhaps we ought not to complain, for I am sure we are quite as different from our grandmothers as they are from theirs.'

'I am afraid I am ·degenerate enough to be glad of the difference. The days when one travelled post must have been very long ones ; riding on a pillion, as I dare say Dame Cicely did, was better ; still an express train is a pleasanter mode of transit than either. Rupert always laughs at me for my horror of slow trains.'

'I think we live at express speed now,' said Cicely, smiling, 'and of course it affects all classes ; but there is one thing which is the greatest improvement, people are beginning to see the necessity of bestirring themselves, if they would keep up the existing order of things at all. If every one was only alive to their own responsibilities, it would be more hopeful ; but the time may come for that yet. And the age is certainly getting highly instructed—witness school-children learning the " Lady of the Lake,"—so I hope education in its true sense will follow. But I am teasing you with my sententious remarks, Lady Mortimer ; it is a favourite hobby of mine to speculate on the possibilities of improvement, and runs away with me. I was wanting to tell you also how glad I am to hear that Mr. Percival is going to stand for Cheston, when there is a vacancy. I hope you are a keen politician.'

'Oh, red-hot !' exclaimed Winnie, laughing. 'But I really must go now ; it is getting quite late. Thank you so much for all you have told me, Miss Royle. I shall soon come and invade you again.'

' I shall be delighted at the invasion.' And
Cicely Royle and Winifred Mortimer
parted mutually pleased with each other;
while the latter thought as she rode home,
' If Cicely with all her suffering, and not
able to move, does so much for others, what
ought not I to do, who have so many opportunities ?' And she mused over the subject,
and longed to do her own duty well, deeply
feeling that life is given us for something
higher than a mere round of pleasure.

·▲

CHAPTER V.

LORD CLANVILLE.

'The woman's cause is man's : they rise or sink
Together, dwarf'd or godlike, bond or free :

    *   *   *   *   *   *

      Let her make herself her own
To give or keep, to live and learn and be
All that not harms distinctive womanhood.
For woman is not undeveloped man,
But diverse : could we make her as the man,
Sweet Love were slain : his dearest bond is this—
Not like to like, but like in difference.'

                              TENNYSON.

AT the beginning of February Lord and Lady Mortimer went up to London for a few days for the meeting of Parliament. The weather was bitterly cold, and London was in a garb of grey snow when they arrived; for, even as they fall, the pure white snow-flakes acquire a leaden hue in floating down through the fog and smoke of a winter's day, to repose on the black mud of London streets. Snow is dreary everywhere, but especially snow in London.

A country landscape is very pretty in its garb of pure white, with heavily-laden trees looking rather as if they found the wintry covering too cumbersome to support, and cottages whose thatch and slates are alike disguised under the white roofs which look so substantial.

But even in the country the eye is soon tired of the general whiteness, and longs for a return of green grass and bare trees; and still sooner does the Londoner desire the disappearance of the discoloured compound, to which even mud alone is preferable.

And when the discomfort of a thaw has passed away, there is a general sensation of relief; for even those who like cold are not partial to snow, and people always grumble at a long spell of cold weather, unless it is of that bright frosty kind which is but rarely seen in England now.

Of course when milder weather succeeds the cold, that will in its turn be pronounced unseasonable; but it would be hard to grudge to Englishmen and Englishwomen their time-honoured privilege of grumbling at the weather, and it must be owned that, considering what the climate of 'merry England' is, there is some cause of complaint.

Though the word climate hardly describes weather in England, for, as a distinguished American once said when asked what he thought of the English climate :

' There is no climate, but a great deal of changeable weather.'

And so Parliament met ; there were the usual addresses on the Queen's speech, and the usual complaints from the opposition that the said speech was totally barren of information, and that it omitted to notice any of the most needed measures of legislation, complaints which have been made with unfailing regularity as each session began, and which, curiously enough, recur without any regard as to which party is in power and which in opposition. For however desirous of information the party out of office may be, no sooner have they succeeded to power than their reticence equals that of their opponents.

A few days after the meeting of Parliament, Lord Mortimer, who was much interested in bringing in a bill intended to promote the improvement of the dwelling-houses of the poorer classes, spoke in the House of Lords on some question connected with it. His speech was a good one, and was much spoken of; and the night after, at a small dinner-party in Grosvenor Place, where the Mortimers' town-house was, Lord Clanville, a member of the Government, came to Winnie and congratulated her warmly on it.

'We were delighted with Mortimer's speech,' said he; 'it was clear, well-worded, and to the point—a very important item! and this bill which he has brought in, about the artisans' dwelling-houses, will be a great improvement if it passes, and I think it will pass. Do you take any interest in politics, Lady Mortimer?'

'Yes, a great deal of interest,' was her

answer. ' I am afraid I don't know as much about them as I ought; but I am learning to understand them better.'

' I am very glad to hear it; it always provokes me when ladies take no interest in their husbands' political views. According to my old-fashioned ideas, a wife ought to help her husband as far as she is able in whatever line he may take; and that would be a better occupation, to my mind, than haranguing meetings and working for woman's suffrage, as is the great aim of strong-minded women now. Have you been to hear Miss Clacker ?'

' No, indeed I have no curiosity; and if I had, I am sure my husband would not let me go. I read her speech through, and thought it was great rubbish; and I never shall believe in lady doctors.'

' Nor I,' replied Lord Clanville; ' and these

public speakers neglect all a woman's natural duties. So far, perhaps, I ought not to be too hard on them, for I suspect they generally belong to the class of women who have failed in the first object of their lives—matrimony. Their abuse of men always reminds me of a fable concerning sour grapes.'

'How angry they would be if they heard you,' said Winnie, laughing. 'You know they profess to be far superior to all considerations of that kind, and I believe look on all married women who do not adopt their ideas with contemptuous pity ; well, I for one can survive it. Of course there are a great many women who have to earn their own living, and find it hard work to decide on some occupation. I am very sorry for them; but I think, if they would undertake less ambitious employment, they would get on better. However, ambition is a temptation to a woman always, I suppose ; and it is quite useless to us, though most useful to men.'

' Why should ambition be quite useless to women ?' asked Lord Clanville. ' Certainly their ambition ought to be of a different kind to a man's ; they should not desire to be lord chancellors, and they need not particularly wish for the toils of cabinet ministers '—and he gave a little expressive shrug of his shoulders— ' but they may be ambitious of helping their husbands and ordering their households well, and of making themselves useful in raising the tone of society, and helping to support measures calculated to improve those around them. And if a woman is unmarried, there are plenty of ways in which she can make herself useful. But dear me, in these days a woman's only ambition, in society at least, seems to be to get herself talked about. I know you are not one of that sort, Lady

Mortimer; and, as an old man, I should like to give you a piece of advice. You are in a position in which you can set an example in society. Do set your face against these fast ways of young married women, and show that you may be lively, fashionable, and useful, without being either fast or strong-minded. There, what a lecture I am giving you! You'll think me worse than Miss Clacker, and certainly I am suggesting a career to you. But I often think I should have more hope for the country than I have at present, if I could see the women of the upper classes think of something else besides amusing themselves, regardless of their duties and responsibilities.'

'You are quite right, Lord Clanville. I only wish I could come up to my ideal of what a woman ought to do when she has any position or responsibility.'

' The very wish makes me sure you will do
something,' he gallantly replied. 'There, Mortimer,' as Lord Mortimer came towards them,
' your wife and I have been having a grand
discussion, and she is quite willing to undertake the task of reforming society—no easy
one, I'm afraid. Indeed,' as Winnie moved
to say good-bye to another of her guests, ' I
congratulate you on having got a wife of the
right sort. Well, things are bad enough ;
and, old Tory though I am, I've got a good
deal of the Reformer in me, eh !'

' The best combination,' answered Lord
Mortimer. ' I always think the only chance
against the ever-growing Radicalism of our
day, is for the Tories to undertake the task
of Reform themselves ; and I don't mean
by Reform, the Reform Bill alone.'

' No, no, of course not ; you and I think
alike about these things. Well, I look on you

as my pupil, you know, Mortimer; and I hope one day to see you in the cabinet, and your wife doing the society part, which we want done so much, and which my good friend Lady Lister has not the smallest idea of accomplishing. Could anything be duller than her drum last Saturday. Well, good-bye, Lady Mortimer, don't forget your mission ;' and Lord Clanville took his departure.

'What a dear old man he is !' said Winnie to her husband, when her other guests were gone ; 'one feels such a respect for him too, when one thinks of his steady, straightforward course all through his long political life.'

' He is one in a thousand,' said Lord Mortimer warmly, 'and all the trouble of his own life—for you know his wife, to whom he was devoted, only lived two years after their marriage—has only made him more sympathising and considerate to others. He is really like a man in days " when none were for a party, but all were for the state," and his great object all through has been not his own advancement, but the welfare of his country and of his countrymen.'

Most true were the words, and justly honoured amongst all good men was Lord Clanville; though full seventy years old, his form was still upright, and the noble face, to which his grey hairs gave additional dignity, bore on it the stamp of a good conscience.

We may be thankful that there are such men in England, honourable, high-minded, and patriotic, and that in all parties we recognise them, and rejoice that English statesmen should, however much they may differ as to the means, honestly desire and strive for their country's good as their end.

And Winnie remembered Lord Clanville's

words, and often thought of them. She fully felt that hers was a great responsibility. Life was opening before her, and she had everything which a woman could wish for. Her husband, to whom she was devoted, possessed not only rank and wealth, but talent and influence, and was, above all, anxious to employ his possessions for the good of others. She herself had youth and health, and personal attractions, though without pretensions to beauty. And, as has been said, life was before her—life with its infinite possibilities of pleasure, excitement: of honour, fame, and power: and those things which duty called on her to undertake were the things to which she was naturally drawn by inclination. To a keen love of art and beauty was joined the full power of enjoying these things in the pleasantest and easiest way ; and as Winnie contrasted her own lot in life with that of others whom she knew, and especially with that of Mary and Cicely Royle, she could only feel intense thankfulness and humility that she should have so much and they so little. She never imagined that life would have no cares or troubles for her ; but she felt deeply how high her aims ought to be, while her opportunities were so great, and how complete her fulfilment of them.

The next day she went to see a cousin of hers, who devoted most of her life to working amongst the London poor, visiting the hospitals and other charitable institutions, and had a long conversation with her respecting her labours.

Mrs. Vincent, the lady in question, was a widow, without children and comfortably off, living in a small house in Belgravia. She had a very sweet attractive face, and possessed in a high degree the gift of sympathy, which, combined as it was in her with good judgment and good sense, made her specially suited to the work she had undertaken. She was very glad to find that her bright young cousin was anxious to join in the much-needed occupation of helping others ; and while she cautioned her against embarking in any new schemes of charity without consideration, gave her much information about the different kinds of aid which were most useful to the London poor.

'Though I often think, Winnie,' she said, 'that one is apt to forget that there are other people who want help besides the very poor. I have a great theory about doing something to cheer and enliven the lives of those who, while they have just enough to live on, have nothing to spare for making life pleasant. For instance, there are two old maiden ladies, sisters, whom I know, living in a very poor

little lodging ; they have bad health, and
hardly enough to live on.   I go and see them
when I can, and take them some flowers or
fruit sometimes, or an amusing book ; and
they are so cheered by any little attention.   I
shall ask you to make their acquaintance when
you are settled in London, for an occasional
visit would be the greatest kindness.   Things
like that cost so little, and are worth so
much.   Were there ever truer lines written
than—

> ' " Evil is wrought
> By want of thought——"

I am quite sure if people thought of these
little things they would do them; but they live
in a whirl, and never think.'

'It is quite true, Cousin Lucy.   I shall be
very glad to go and see your old ladies.   When
one is as happy as I am, it makes one feel so
sorry for those whose lives seem to be all

sorrow. And there is such a fearful amount of misery in the world, it makes everything that can be done to alleviate it seem almost useless, when one thinks of the remainder that cannot be touched by any efforts whatever.'

'The only hope is, for every one to do what they can,' answered Mrs. Vincent; 'and first of all to try and keep one's own standard high, and never neglect the little daily duties of life. I can't tell you, Winnie, how glad I am that you care about something else besides amusement; and you have the greatest help in a husband like Lord Mortimer.'

'Indeed I have!' exclaimed the happy young wife. 'Oh, he is the very best of men! I do pity girls, Cousin Lucy, who can't look up to their husbands; it must be dreadful. I don't know what would become of me, if I could not feel that my husband was in every way above me.'

Mrs. Vincent smiled ; her inward thought was that Winnie herself was too high-minded ever to have married any man who was not her superior, but she only said :

'Well, it is a good thing every one does not think alike in those respects; and love very often makes girls believe in the superiority of men who are in reality their inferiors.'

'Well, perhaps so ; but I never could have married a man I did not respect.'

'No, Winnie, I don't think you could. I felt the same, and had the same happiness of a good husband that you have. But every one is not so fortunate ;' and she gave a little sigh, as her thoughts wandered back over her ten years' widowhood, and fifteen years' happy married life.

But Lucy Vincent had been too thankful for happiness to repine at sorrow ; and if she felt that the sunshine of her own life had departed on the day when her idolised husband was taken from her, her one aim since had been to try to lead a life which might be useful to others. She was too humble-minded to know how well she had succeeded. Truly her sorrow had been blessed to many around her.

When Winnie returned home, she found her brother Geoffrey waiting for her.

'I wanted to have a talk with you, Winnie,' he said. 'Had you any idea that there was anything going on between Vernon and Kitty.'

Quickly as thought could come, flashed across Winnie the recollection of her husband's suspicions, and she exclaimed hurriedly :

'Oh, surely not, Geoffrey? I do hope there is nothing. I know she liked dancing with him, but then——' and she stopped.

'It is quite true. I went home for two days, in fact I only returned this morning, and Vernon went with me. Well, last night he proposed to Kitty, and she, as far as she is concerned, accepted him; but of course afterwards, when he had an interview with my father, it was found that his means are desperately small. He has only two hundred a year, besides his pay; and his regiment is going to India almost immediately. He behaved very well about it, and owned that he had no right to think of Kitty, excepting that of being quite devoted to her, and threw himself on my father's mercy.'

'And what did he say?' asked Winnie, breathlessly.

'That, considering how young Kitty is, he could not possibly sanction any engagement; and that, though he had no objection to him personally, he could not let Kitty marry without a sufficient income. So it is all at an end, as far as any engagement goes ; but I don't think they will either of them change their minds. And that reminds me, isn't Cis's old cousin, Miss Haleswell, a neighbour of yours ?'

'Yes, certainly she is ; but what has that to do with it ? Oh, I see,' as it suddenly dawned on her, ' you are thinking she might do something for him. Do you know, Geoffrey, it would not surprise me at all ; she talked to me of him, and seemed very fond of him.'

'Yes, she is ; but Cis is no fortune-hunter, and he can't bear to think of counting on the old lady's will. He never said a syllable to my father about her, so of course I could not ; and he is very low about it altogether, for if she does nothing for him, he has no other prospects.'

' Surely he might tell Miss Haleswell that he likes Kitty, only he can't afford to marry her ?'

' So I think ; but he says it would look like asking for a settlement. I was wondering if you could throw in a hint when you see her, Winnie ?'

' I am afraid it would be difficult, as Kitty would be the gainer. Oh, here's Rupert; I may tell him, Geoffrey ?'

' Oh, certainly !'

And she recounted the history to her husband, adding :

' You were quite right, Rupert, in thinking that Kitty liked him.'

' Had you any suspicions, Mortimer ?' asked Geoffrey.

' Yes, I had ; and, as it turns out, my suspicions were right. It is unfortunate, though, about the money ; and his heirship to Miss Haleswell is very uncertain.'

'You do think it possible?' said his wife.

'I have always considered it so ; but, Geoffrey, Vernon had better tell her the whole story.'

'Exactly what I say,' was the response 'but he's afraid she will think he's after her money.'

'No fear of that ; she knows him too well. I don't say she may not have had other views for his marrying, but that is nothing now. And, if he wanted fortune, there was Miss Ashby ready to hand—was there not, Winnie ?'

'Oh, Rupert, it was so stupid of me to make such a mistake ; but, having done it,' I should be delighted if there was any prospect of all this coming to a satisfactory conclusion.'

'You see,' remarked Geoffrey, 'it is not only that Vernon is my dearest friend, but

Kitty is my sister, and I should be uncommonly pleased at their marriage. Besides, I feel rather guilty, for I knew he liked her, and certainly did not put obstacles in the way of their meeting, which perhaps, knowing he was poor, I ought to have done ; but I let it go, and am sorry enough now. Poor Kitty is dreadfully unhappy, and my father and mother too ; you'll hear it all from them to-morrow, Winnie, but I told them I should come and tell you the whole history.'

'I'm so glad you did,' answered his sister ; 'but I only wish it could have a happier termination.'

'There can be no doubt that Cis Vernon had better tell Miss Haleswell the state of the case,' said Lord Mortimer. 'Whether or not she means to make him her heir, she is so straightforward that she will let him know what her intentions are, when she hears of his contemplating a marriage. I am sorry for Kitty, for anyway it must be a long waiting, as Cis has to go to India so soon.'

'Well,' replied Geoffrey, rising to go, 'I shall do my utmost to persuade Cis to tell Miss Haleswell about it when he goes to say good-bye to her, in a day or two, and I hope something may come of it.'

CHAPTER VI.

MISS HALESWELL'S HEIR.

'There's nothing half so sweet in life
As Love's young dream.'

WHEN Geoffrey was gone, Lord Mortimer would have been more than human if he had not again recurred to the justice of his discernment.

'Well, Winnie,' he said, 'I am sorry that my suspicions were correct; but, you see, I was right in thinking that Kitty liked Vernon.'

There is a delightful sensation, to which

every one is liable, in feeling that something which we have predicted, and which no one else has believed in, has yet been proved to be true, and the best of us cannot resist the temptation of alluding to their own superior foresight when their prediction is verified : nor is it easy to conceal one's vexation when one finds one's self wrong, after having, perhaps, shown great confidence in one's own judgment; and Winnie certainly felt rather provoked that her husband should have discovered what she had been blind to.

'Yes, I acknowledge you were right, Rupert ; but it is very odd that you should have been,' she said. 'I thought men never saw things of that sort ; no doubt I should have found it out if I had thought more about it.' But Winnie quite forgot that it was because she had thought so much of her

own match-making plans for her guests
that she had failed to observe the matches
which were making themselves.

' If Miss Haleswell does something for
Vernon, it may come all right,' went on
Lord Mortimer, forbearing to tease his wife
any more about her lack of observation ; ' but
anyhow they will have to wait, which is
never a good thing. Long engagements are
very trying to both parties.'

' Indeed they are, and I should be sorry
for Kitty to have to undergo the weary
waiting of one. Even you, Rupert, though
you dislike match-making, must allow that it
would have been far better if Kitty could
have liked the Duke of Trent.'

' Of course, it would have been a very
good marriage for her; but I don't feel sure
that it would have at all suited Kitty to be
a duchess. And Vernon is a very good

fellow. We must hope it will come right; but India would be another drawback, in your father's opinion, I suppose?'

'I am afraid so; though I can never quite make out why people have such an aversion to their daughters going to India.'

'I think I can,' said Lord Mortimer, 'when I look at those who have gone to India as bright healthy girls, and returned worn-out women, with their health ruined, their spirits gone.'

'Oh, Rupert, that is a very black view. India does not ruin everybody's health.'

'Not everybody's, of course; but I think few Englishwomen pass through the Indian climate unscathed. However, if Kitty cares enough for Vernon to go to India with him, I hope she may be able to do so; for there is nothing I dislike more than the prevailing notion, that if a man in the army marries, he must exchange, or sell out, directly his regiment is ordered to India.   After all, a wife's place is with her husband, whenever she can be with him without interfering with his duties ; and it is a sad pity when a woman takes it into her head that her husband should give up his profession because he has married her.   She should have asked herself what she was prepared to give up for him before she married him.   I cannot understand how women can act in such a selfish manner, when they so often by it ruin their husband's best prospects, and of course, with those, injure eventually their own interest.   Though, in one sense, it is a man's own fault for giving into such a thing, nor can I conceive why any one does it.   I suppose I have too much of the tyrant in me to be so yielding.'

'A great deal too much,' laughed his wife, 'as I shall find if I am late for dinner; so I must go and dress now, to ensure punctuality.'

Two days after, Cis Vernon found himself in the train, *en route* to Miss Haleswell's. He felt very wretched as he thought of his future prospects. He was very much in love with Kitty, and very miserable at the thought of leaving England without any hope of winning her; and yet he felt not only reluctant to tell Miss Haleswell of his trouble, but the reverse of hopeful as to her helping him even if she knew of it; so he was very down-hearted and unlike himself when he arrived, as his cousin soon discovered.'

'Now, Cis,' she said, when they were sitting together in the evening, 'I am sure there is something wrong with you. Tell me all about your troubles, and let me see if I

can help you, so that you may not go to
India with any debts or worries on your
mind.'

'You are very good, Emma,' he said, and
he stood up leaning against the high oak
mantelpiece with a very despondent air; 'but
it is not debt or anything of that sort.'

'Then it is a love affair, Cis,' said the old
lady, who was keen-sighted enough to guess
at the state of the case.

'Yes, it is; and as you've guessed it, I'll
tell you the whole history,' said Cis, very
much relieved at the ice being broken, and
feeling it a comfort to pour out his heart to
his kind-hearted listener. 'The fact is, I
proposed the other day to Miss de Valines—
Kitty. And she's the dearest girl in the world,
and likes me; but her father, I can't blame
him, says he can't consent to my marrying
her without more money than I shall ever

have. So it's all over, and I don't know what's to become of me, neither do I much care. I shall be off to India in a week, and never see her or hear of her again, until some day she marries some lucky dog with money, who won't care for her half as much as I do; for I have no right to expect she'll remember me.'

Cecil Vernon's confession was certainly not distinguished for its eloquence, but the real feeling which he showed touched the warm heart of Miss Haleswell, and though for a moment she felt a sensation of disappointment that her scheme for his marrying Lilian Royle must now be at an end, when he had finished, she said:

'Now, Cis, listen to me, and perhaps I can help you in this. I won't deny that I have wished that you might take a fancy to another girl, who shall be nameless now, but

I'm the last person in the world to wish people to marry unless they love each other. I don't forget my own young days, though they are so long ago, and therefore I think I had better tell you now what my intentions about you are, and perhaps they may forward your marriage. My fortune, Cis, stood in the way of my happiness when I was young, but it will be some consolation to me if by it I can secure yours now. I have always meant you to be my heir; you are my nearest relation, and I shall settle the estate on you at once, and allow you five hundred pounds a year as long as I live. No, stop,' as he was going to speak; 'I have not finished yet. This would not give you a large income at present, but with your own two hundred and your pay, I think it might be sufficient to make a difference in Colonel de Valines's ultimatum; so I shall write him a letter stating my intentions, as I have told them to you, and give it you either to take or send it to him. Your departure being so near will probably oblige you to have a long engagement; but, if I am right, I think even that at the present time would rejoice your heart.'

'I should think so!' exclaimed Cis. 'Oh, you dear good Emma, how can I ever thank you enough! You will believe me when I tell you that I never expected such a thing; it is indeed happiness to think that I may win Kitty yet, for her father is not unreasonable, so I am sure your letter will amply satisfy him. I can never repay you for your goodness—nor Kitty either,' he added.

'Indeed you both can; you will be the children of my old age. And when you come back from India, you must look on Elm Court as your home. Why, Cis, you will perhaps get the better of old Bacon, who is more obstinate than ever when I suggest any improvements; and Kitty, for so I must call her, will help me in making the house pleasant when I get dull and infirm.'

'The idea of your getting dull! Well, I can only thank you again and again, and say if only we can in any way show you our gratitude, we shall do so.'

'I know it, Cis; there, don't say any more. I shall long for the time when you and your wife come home to Elm Court.'

And warm-hearted Miss Haleswell rejoiced that she had it in her power to make two young lives happy; her own sad love-story had made her very considerate for the loves of others, and, unlike many old maids, she did all in her power to encourage marriage amongst her friends and acquaintances.

The sequel to this conversation may easily

be imagined. When Cis Vernon left Elm Court, he went at once to Skeatings; and after a long interview with Colonel de Valines, in which he detailed to him the whole of Miss Haleswell's generous proposals, ending with giving him her letter, he found that gentleman willing to allow his engagement to Kitty.

'As a rule, Vernon,' said the colonel, who was by no means a representative of the mercenary father type, 'I can't say I approve of long engagements, or of letting girls go to India, but yet I am giving my consent to both. The truth is that Kitty, though she has been very good in submitting to my fiat, has been so miserable since I gave it, that I felt as if I was very cruel towards her; and I am very glad that your cousin's kindness has enabled me to revoke my prohibition, for I believe you will do your utmost to take care

of her, and to make her happy.   So you
may go and tell Kitty that I withdraw my
objections ; you will find her in the morning-
room.'

It is needless to say that Cis's interview
with Kitty was a very satisfactory one, and
as she raised her blue eyes to him, she said :

'Oh, Cis, it seems too wonderful ! to think
how miserable I was ten days ago, and now
it is all right, and we belong to each other !'

'It is perfect happiness,' was his answer.
'Oh, my darling, how can I ever show you
how grateful I am to you for consenting, in
spite of a long engagement, to give yourself
to me !'

'A long engagement is better than a long
parting, Cis,' was her reply.   And in their
new-found happiness they found consolation
for the separation so close on them, for Cis
Vernon sailed for India four days afterwards,

with no expectation of returning before two years; and then he was to return to England on leave, and take Kitty back with him as his bride.

Kitty de Valines was young, but her disposition was a sunny one, and she prepared herself bravely to face the two long years.

'After all,' she said to herself, 'I shall not be much over twenty then, and in these two years I will try my utmost to learn to be a useful wife to Cis. Oh, that dear good Miss Haleswell, if it had not been for her, what would my feelings have been! then I should have had no hope to cheer me, and I could not do without some hope.'

Soon after Kitty went to visit Miss Haleswell, and the old lady and the young girl became fast friends, and the visit was often repeated. Kitty made acquaintance with Elm Court and its surroundings, and was initiated into all Miss Haleswell's hobbies and schemes of improvement. She won golden opinions, and even took old Bacon the bailiff's heart by storm, not a very easy triumph, for that worthy belonged to the school of cantankerous individuals who always oppose everything that they do not originate, and as they rarely originate anything, their opposition becomes almost universal, and poor Miss Haleswell generally found herself quite unequal to overcoming the prejudices of her bailiff, who styled the simplest improvements 'new-fangled nonsense,' and generally contrived that the 'new-fangled nonsense' should prove a failure for lack of being properly used. So passed the first part of Kitty's two years' engagement.

CHAPTER VII.

GEOFFREY'S PURCHASE.

'Oh, beautiful creature, what am I
    That I dare to look her way,
    o   o   o   o   o
    And dream of her beauty with tender dread?'
                                                TENNYSON.

SOME few days after Cis Vernon had found himself declared the heir of Elm Court, and thereby enabled to engage himself to Kitty de Valines, Miss Haleswell drove over to Royle Abbey to tell her friends there the news. She only found Cicely at home, and after paying her a long visit, and lingering on in the hopes of seeing Mary and Lilian, she at last took her leave, saying she must wait no longer. She had hardly been gone ten minutes before Lilian made her appearance in her habit.

'Oh, Lilian!' exclaimed her sister, 'you are just too late; Miss Haleswell has been here, and she was so anxious to see you, but could not wait any longer. She came to announce a piece of news : Captain Vernon is engaged to Miss Kitty de Valines, and she has decided on making him heir to Elm Court; he is going—indeed I believe is gone —to India, so it will be a long engagement.'

'You don't say so!' answered Lilian, subsiding into an arm-chair by her sister's couch ; 'well, I am quite surprised, but it is a very good thing. Does Miss Haleswell like it ?'

'She seems delighted. By the way, there is a letter for you ; I think it is from John.'

Lilian took up the envelope, and began to read her letter. Cicely watched her anxiously, for John Royle's epistles were not always causes of rejoicing to his sisters, and she trembled lest it should contain some injunctions to induce his father to send him some money. So it was with a sense of relief that she heard her sister say, as she handed her the letter:

'There's not much in it; John is coming down to-morrow, and going to bring Mr. de Valines, who wants to have a look at that black horse which the dear old padre wishes to sell.'

Cicely read over the lines, and noticed that John, too, mentioned the engagement Miss Haleswell had just been telling her of, and remarked:

'John seems to see a good deal of Mr. de Valines; I am so glad, for they are all such good people, and he is said to be such a nice young fellow.'

' He's very pleasant,' said Lilian, carelessly. ' There, I must really go and take off my habit ;' and she disappeared, certainly not ill-pleased at the information her brother's letter contained.

Poor Cicely! she little thought, as she rejoiced over John's having some nice friends, that he was too thoroughly worthless to be improved by any companions, or indeed to care about the society of any excepting the wild, fast set to which he belonged, and she never dreamed that his friendship was generally fatal to any young man who might be unfortunate enough to fall under his influence. In the present case, he would hardly have obtained so much hold over Geoffrey de Valines in such a short space of time, had it not been that Geoffrey was so entirely infatuated by Lilian's beauty, that he hoped by cultivating her brother's acquaintance he might get more chance of seeing her, more especially as, deceived by the affectionate manner in which John Royle spoke of his family, he believed that he spent much time with them, which was certainly not the case. And Geoffrey hailed with delight the proffer to come down and inspect a horse which Sir Hugh was anxious to sell.

Mary Royle soon came in from a round of parish visits, and the next minute in bustled Sir Hugh.

'I have just been hearing,' he began, 'that that Ned Shaw has been poaching again, trapping rabbits this time. That man is an utter scoundrel; he will come to the gallows in time. I am afraid Sparks does not half look after the lower plantation; I have given him a good scolding about it. I only wish we could catch the rascal;' and Sir Hugh paused, while Mary said :

' Oh, I am so sorry for his poor wife.   She is so ill, and he is out of work again.'

' More shame to him, my dear ; more shame to him.   I am sorry for his wife, but she should look after him more ; and as to work, who would employ a poacher ?'

' No ´ one, I am afraid,' answered his daughter.

' Quite right too ; it would be encouraging vice,' said Sir Hugh, virtuously, as became a landlord, a magistrate, and preserver of game, to whom poachers were as a red rag to a bull, and by whom they were regarded as guilty of the worst crimes.   Indeed, it is almost amusing sometimes to hear the condemnation of any luckless family whose members are known as poachers ; if there are any steady ones amongst the number, they will hardly get the credit of being so. And indeed, as a rule in the country, the habitual poachers are amongst the wildest and most lawless of the inhabitants of a place. Whether they become so by poaching, or whether, being wild and lawless, they take to poaching as the most exciting employment within their reach, is a doubtful point ; but it is certainly extraordinary that while the land-owners not unnaturally look on it as a desperate crime, the poor, even though honest and respectable, cannot be brought to regard it as any other than a venial offence ; and while they would be horrified at the idea of taking your purse, yet have no objection to a hare or so being secured now and then by their mankind—accidentally of course.

The Royles were well accustomed to hear Sir Hugh's tirades against Ned Shaw and his belongings, and Cicely, not anxious to prolong the discussion, told of Miss Haleswell's visit and news, and of John's intended visit.

Sir Hugh was much interested in the engagement, for he was one of those men who delighted in hearing of cheerful events, and marriages he regarded as coming into that category.

'So John is going to bring young De Valines down to see about that horse,' he remarked, after he had discussed the other news; 'well, he's a beauty. I wish I could keep him, but horses won't live on air, and we've got as many as we can keep—properly speaking, more—without him. I suppose, though, that the Mortimers are not yet back by this, otherwise De Valines would have gone to his sister's.' Sir Hugh said this, quite unsuspecting what attraction Royle Abbey held for Geoffrey.

'No,' answered Cicely, ' I don't think they are coming back to the castle till next week : they are staying in London longer than they intended to do ;' a fact of which John Royle was also aware, for, conscious of Lord Mortimer's estimation of him, and cordially hating him, he did not wish to endanger the success of his schemes by bringing his intercourse with Geoffrey before the keen eyes of the earl.

So, on the evening of the next day, John Royle and his companion arrived. Sir Hugh gave Geoffrey a hearty greeting, and Lilian certainly did not appear displeased to see him ; while John played his game most skilfully, and contrived, by interesting his father in the latest political news and by giving his sisters some amusing accounts of various friends, that Geoffrey and Lilian should have a good deal of conversation

together. Later on, Sir Hugh, who was
very fond of music, asked Lilian for some
of his favourite songs. Lilian did not
possess any remarkable gift of voice, but
she sang simple airs, and old English or
quaint French songs, with great sweetness
and expression, and perhaps her singing was
more calculated to give pleasure to her
listeners than if she had entertained them
with the most classic German melodies. For
excepting to people who are not only
thoroughly musical, but who really understand classical music, that kind of music in
the evening is not always a source of delight.
After dinner the generality of men and
women like to be amused, and, though a
truly classical musician will scorn the idea,
absolutely prefer the so-called inferior music
of England and Italy to the most exquisite
compositions of Wagner. In fact (shades of

German composers, what will you say to it?)
one does hear a hunting song, or even one
from an *opéra bouffe*, meet with approval
and applause which are conspicuously absent
when the higher style of music is the order
of the evening.

Nor is there anything surprising in this;
the same people who like light music in the
evening may be perfectly able to enjoy
scientific music at its proper time, but in
society in the evening they would be equally
indisposed to listen to a scientific lecture, or
to go deeply into some abstruse question
on art or politics. And it is a great pity
that real musicians, while doing all in their
power to raise the general appreciation of
good music, should despise the lighter kinds
of it, which do not pretend to rival the
higher, and only intend to amuse and not to
instruct the listeners.

Most certainly Sir Hugh infinitely preferred 'John Anderson, my Jo,' 'Robin
Adair,' and his well-beloved 'John Peel,'
to anything superior; and as for Geoffrey de
Valines, he began to think that Lilian
Royle's voice was as sweet as Patti's. For
as we all know that love is blind, so we may
also presume that love plays tricks with our
faculties of hearing, as there is no other
way of accounting for the different opinions
expressed as to a young lady's voice by her
admirers, and by her rivals.

So passed the evening, very agreeably to
all the party; and the next day Sir Hugh,
John Royle, and Lilian, with Geoffrey de
Valines, proceeded to inspect the black horse
whose wonderful beauty and promise were
of course the only inducements for the young
guardsman's visit.

It was a bright frosty morning, with that

peculiar clearness and brilliant blue sky which one sometimes, not often now, sees in an English winter day. The stables at Royle had formed part of the buildings belonging to the original abbey, and were very picturesque, looking especially so as they stood up against the clear sky with their red walls tempered with the hue that age gives to red, and which makes old buildings of that colour so different from the modern erections in the same tint. The old gables and quaint archway were duly re- marked by Geoffrey; and, at last, the quartette reached that part of the stables where in all his glory stood the black horse. He was carefully inspected, and greatly admired, and Geoffrey, well pleased with his appearance, decided on purchasing him.

'You have not given him a name yet, have you?' he asked.

'No,' answered Sir Hugh. 'Here, Lilian, you generally give all the horses their names ; suggest some suitable ones for this black beauty.'

'I wish you would,' said Geoffrey, as Lilian paused in consideration, and then answered :

'I think you ought to name him, as he is going to be yours ; however, if you ask me, I think I should call him "Rob Roy," for he looks as if he had plenty of pluck, a quality which I am afraid in Rob Roy himself makes me forget his disregard of the laws of *meum* and *tuum.*'

'It is a capital name,' said Geoffrey. 'Rob Roy let him be. I am delighted with my new acquisition.'

'Will you come and see the oldest inhabitant of the place, Mr. de Valines ?' asked Lilian. 'A very important person, I

assure you, and one who always expects a
visit from every stranger who comes to the
stables.'

He willingly assented, as she laughingly
led the way to another part of the stables,
and opening a low door, said, with mock
reverence :

'Let me introduce you to my dear old
pony Peggy.'

The pony in question was a grey one, un-
deniably a very ancient lady, but who showed
great delight at seeing her young mistress ;
and her delight was not lessened when she
munched the lumps of sugar with which
Lilian liberally supplied her.

'Peggy is a wonderful creature,' said
the young lady, as she fed her favourite.
'She is past thirty, certainly, and we all
learnt to ride on her. I rode her at four
years old, and continued to do so as long as

she could carry me. She was a capital jumper, and I had my first day's hunting on her. Dear old thing! one gets so fond of animals when they are old friends, don't you think so ?'

' Indeed I quite agree with you. They are such faithful friends, too—that is to say, dogs and horses are, which are the kind of animals I know most about.'

' And they are so superior to the rest, that they ought not to be classed with other animals. Ah, there goes one of another species for which I have no partiality,' as a huge sandy cat walked demurely past them. ' I cannot endure pet cats. There is an old woman in this village who owns nine, and whenever I go to see her, I always say, " Now, please, Mrs. Bartlett, come away from all your precious cats, for I am come to see you, not them." '

'I should think she was rather indignant with you, for disliking her pets.'

'Oh, she gets very angry, and we have a grand quarrel; and then make it up, till next time.'

Then they walked leisurely back across the old bridge over the stream which flowed between the house and the stables, and rambled round the old-fashioned flower-garden. It was winter now, and therefore there was nothing to see in it; but in summer, though Royle was not remarkable for the splendour of its flowers, it was the most delightful old garden in the world. All the sweet-scented flowers, which one misses so much amid the blaze of colour which rejoices the eye in the wonderfully-shaped bed of a modern parterre, might be found there in plenty. Indeed the garden at Royle was one which existed for pleasure, and not for show ; and, without saying a word against show-gardens, one may be allowed to indulge in a preference for a place where one may gather a nosegay of sweet flowers without incurring thereby the wrath of a grand gardener.

Geoffrey de Valines thought with regret how short his visit must be, and, anxious to be sure of future meetings with Lilian, said, as they neared the house after their walk :

'I suppose you will come up to London after Easter ?'

'Oh no, I don't think so ; at least, not regularly.   We never have gone up for the season, only for two or three weeks at the end of May.'

'But then you are out now,' persisted Geoffrey ; 'so I should think Sir Hugh will take you up for some gaieties.'

'I hardly think he will, though I am

sure I should like it immensely. Still my father does not care for London for long; and then Cicely could not go, so I shall have to content myself with a country cousin's fortnight;' and she laughed merrily, not seeming much distressed at the idea.

Geoffrey was by no means pleased at the intelligence, for he had been looking forward to seeing much of Lilian during the season, and had very definite ideas as to his hopes for its close. And now he heard that she would not be in London for more than a short time. He would not, however, give up hope yet.

'Some one is sure to ask you to stay with them,' suggested he.

' Oh, how I wish some one would !' exclaimed Lilian. 'Really you should not put such a notion into my head, for I am afraid there is not the least chance of it.'

'I hope there is a great chance,' answered Geoffrey. 'I—all your friends will regret it if you don't come up for the season.'

'It will be very kind of my friends,' said Lilian, as they entered the hall ; and there was a faint blush on her cheek, for she had heard the 'I' which Geoffrey had so hastily corrected, and was not unwilling to think that future meetings with her present companion might be very pleasant ones.

The afternoon train whirled John Royle and Geoffrey de Valines back to London ; the former well satisfied with the state of affairs, the latter very undecided as to how he should contrive to see Lilian again, but more in love with her than ever, and not without hope that he might win her love in time.

And so for weal or woe Geoffrey de Valines's lot in life was sealed. If he could have lifted the veil which hung over the coming months—if he could have divined the thoughts of John Royle sitting opposite to him in the smoking-carriage, turning over the leaves of a novel which he was not reading— would he have acted differently ?

In one sense he certainly would have done so, but not in another. Knowledge would have saved him from the bitter experience which he had to buy as regarded John Royle ; but as far as Lilian was concerned, he was ready to sacrifice anything for her, and beneath the merry handsome face of the young soldier there was an earnest purpose and a warm heart. Lilian Royle would have reason to be proud of her lover, if circum- stances should come to try his metal ; as yet he was untouched by care or trouble, but when they came he would meet them bravely, and they would teach him much needed lessons. Yes ; careless, gay, *insouciant,* as they seem, there is something deeper in the young men of the present day ; and if trial and danger come, we need not fear that they will be less ready to meet it than their fathers were of old.

CHAPTER VIII.

JOHN ROYLE.

'Knowledge comes, but wisdom lingers, and she bears a laden
    breast
  Full of sad experience, moving towards the stillness of his
    rest.'

TENNYSON.

ON Saturday afternoon, a day or two afterwards, Geoffrey de Valines made his appearance in his sister's drawing-room; and
finding her alone, they settled themselves for
a long conversation. After discussing
Kitty's engagement in all its points, and
various other family news, Geoffrey led the

conversation to matters more personal to himself, by saying :

' Oh, I was down in your neighbourhood two days ago, Winnie. I heard that Sir Hugh Royle had a young horse to sell, and as I was looking out for one, I went there for a night. I purchased the animal in question, and like his looks very much.'

' Oh, did you go to Royle ?' exclaimed his sister ; ' were they all flourishing ? I like the Royles so much l'

' They seemed in very good force,' was his reply. ' Sir Hugh was very hospitable and good-natured, and the young ladies most agreeable. What a charming face the invalid sister has l'

' Indeed she has ; she is a marvel of patience and cheerfulness. I must go over and see them as soon as we go back to Mortimer. I

wonder if they will come to London this
year, now Lilian is out ?'

'I understood not,' remarked Geoffrey
carelessly, as he balanced a paper-knife on
his fingers with remarkable skill. 'Miss
Lilian Royle seemed rather to regret it.'

'Oh, she must wish to come, and being so
lovely she would make quite a sensation.
How I should like to take her out ! I long to
begin chaperoning duties, and am quite
angry with Kitty that she has ceased to
require my services, at least to any great
extent. I wonder whether Rupert would
let me ask Lilian here for a season. I think
I will try and persuade him ; only the worst
is, he cannot endure the brother, Mr.
Royle.'

'But that has nothing to do with your
taking out the sister,' said Geoffrey, only too
delighted that Winnie had herself suggested

the plan : he was longing to propose to her. 'I know there are queer stories of John Royle, but I don't think he's quite as wild as he has been. I should think it would be a kind action if you did ask Miss Lilian Royle for the season. I always pity girls who don't have a little fun in London. What a thing it will be to see you a dignified chaperon, Winnie ! Do you mean to go in for the whole thing, ball-giving and the rest of it ?'

'Yes, I think so. Rupert says I may have a ball if I like, and the room next to this will make a perfect ball-room ; indeed, I think it will be a better plan to have two small dances instead of a big ball—no one can really enjoy a great crush.'

' No, certainly not ; small dances are far pleasanter, and I wish people would think so generally, but I suppose they give more trouble.'

'Not if you have got a room ready to hand, as we have here; besides I do not mind the trouble a bit. If I do give any entertainments, I want them to be successful ones.'

'I think yours are sure to be that, judging by the one at Mortimer.'

'I hope so. Oh, Geoffrey, have you seen anything of the Lyntons?'

'Yes, I came across them at Mrs Delville's drum the other night, and had quite a conversation with Tessie.'

Winnie would have preferred to hear that he had talked to Valla, but was pleased to find he had seen the two sisters, and hoped that her favourite scheme might still come to pass. She was not prepared for her brother's next question.

'Did you know that there was some sort of engagement two years ago between John

Royle and Tessie Lynton, and that Lord Elmarch would not hear of it, on account of his extravagance ?'

'No, indeed I did not,' said she, much interested. 'I wonder if it is really all over.'

'I wonder too, for, casually talking about your neighbours, I found Tessie very keen in her inquiries about the Royles. I did not then know the reason, but chanced to hear it a day or two afterwards.'

Geoffrey did not mention that it was when coming out of Stacy's with John Royle he had seen the Lyntons pass in their victoria, and had noticed the sudden colour on Tessie's face, and the look which passed between her and John Royle. And John Royle's face had changed, and a look of intense admiration had come into his eyes ; and as he walked along by Geoffrey's side he had exclaimed :

'How the sight of that girl maddens me ! if

I had her for my wife, I should be a different man.' Then with a laugh he had changed the subject, and said :

'Well, De Valines, you have seen me in a very unusual mood ; forget it as soon as you can.'

No more had passed, but warm-hearted Geoffrey had felt sincere sympathy with John Royle, and in one sense he was right.

The good point in John Royle's character was his affection for Tessie Lynton ; it was the one thing which gave him some glimpse of better things. If her father had consented to their marriage, would it have reclaimed him? Tessie herself thought so, and though well aware that he was wild and extravagant, would not believe that he was really bad, and grieved bitterly at the thought that she might have made a different man of him if her father would have allowed her to marry him; and she had not forgotten him during the two years which had elapsed since his proposal.

Lord Elmarch's opinion was different, and he and many others, including Lord Mortimer, were convinced that nothing could change John Royle's character.

It is a disputed point whether a good girl can reclaim a bad man, who loves her, by marrying him; but all agree that the risk is a fearful one, and few fathers care to let their daughters run such a risk : though when love is strong in a girl's heart, she feels the almost certain hope that she could keep a man straight as her husband, and the persuasion that loss of her will drive her rejected lover desperate. Sometimes a man may be saved by a wife's influence, but it is not always so, and it is safer and better that a wife should be able to look up to her husband, rather than think that she will be able to guide him when the first glamour of love has passed away.

'Well, Geoffrey,' said his sister, 'you have made me most curious; I wonder if Rupert knows anything of it. The Royles are such old friends of his, that he would have been sure to hear of it; I think I must try and find out.'

'Well, don't betray me; but I thought I would ask you if you had heard of the engagement, Tessie Lynton being a friend of yours.'

'I wonder I did not hear of it; but I suppose, as it was not allowed, they did not talk about it. Can you come to dinner early on Monday, Geoffrey, and go with us to the play? We are going back to Mortimer on Tuesday.'

'I should have liked it very much, but I am engaged to dine with the Tancarvilles. Well, Winnie, I must go now ; and I suppose I shall not see you again, as I shall be on duty on Tuesday : so good-bye.'

Geoffrey de Valines took his leave, well pleased at the results of his interview with his sister, and hoping that the end of her good-natured plan might be that Lilian Royle would be established with her for the season.

Nothing would suit his hopes better ; it would be natural that he should constantly be at his sister's house, and he could then see Lilian without any remark as to his intentions.

'And further,' he said to himself, 'my father can't object to a girl whom Mortimer allows Winnie to have to stay with her ;' for Geoffrey was aware that the name of Royle was not *sans reproche*, and he knew that though, as regarded money, his father would make no objections, he would be far more particular as to the connections and family of his future daughter-in-law.

'Most unlucky,' muttered Geoffrey again, 'that John Royle has got such a bad name; if he would only pull up a little, and marry Tessie Lynton, there would not be an obstacle to my winning Lilian.'

And as he lit his cigar, and wandered on down Piccadilly, he began for the hundredth time to recount to himself Lilian's charms.

And when Lady Mortimer was left alone, she began to consider how best she could gain her husband's consent to chaperoning Lilian Royle. Somehow she instinctively felt that the plan would not meet with his approval, and she was desirous to introduce the subject skilfully, knowing that if he once

said 'no,' he would not change his mind.
For Lord Mortimer, though a most devoted
husband, was very determined, and Winnie
only had her own way in a very modified
degree. Being inclined to be self-willed
herself, Winnie did not always find yielding
pleasant; but she admired her husband incom-
parably more, because she knew that, when
in earnest, his will was law.

So when Lord Mortimer came in that
evening, she did not at once plunge into the
subject of her meditations, but listened to his
news, and the account of a visit to Lord
Clanville, with the latest intelligence respecting the Artisans' Dwelling-houses Bill. Very
pleasant was her interest and enthusiastic
partisanship to her husband, who was a man
who liked women to take interest in politics
and improvements, though strongly opposed
to the so-called 'woman's rights' movement.

And when the lords of the creation really come up to their proper level, and take their standing according to their position and abilities, maintaining their legitimate superiority, it is almost an impossibility for any woman to attempt to vie with them. For woman is 'the second, not the first;' and she will gain far more by filling the second place well, than by attempting to attain to the first place, for which she is not fitted.

On Tuesday the Mortimers returned to Mortimer Castle, and two or three weeks of uninterrupted bad weather prevented Winnie from seeing anything of the Royles, nor did she find an opportunity of mooting her plan about Lilian ; and she finally came to the conclusion that she would say nothing about it until she had herself been to Royle Abbey and found out what its inmates were going to do during the spring and summer.

Indeed, she was too busy to think much about the Royles, for what with helping her husband in his writing and copying, working hard at her own painting, and taking keen interest in the numerous schemes of improvement for the parish, estate and county, in which Lord Mortimer was always engaged, she found her days pass very rapidly; and even when he was out all day, she was not one of those young married women who are a prey to *ennui* directly they are alone.

For why, because a woman is married, should she give up all rational occupations— neglect music, painting, and books—and expect her husband to devote himself to her, to the neglect of more important duties, or else require to be surrounded with a continual succession of guests?

The reason is hard to comprehend. Married women have a sufficient number of advantages, and they make many more for themselves if they only possess the desire to make the best of their position. For every married woman has a position, whether she be a duchess, a member's wife, an officer's bride, or the quiet spouse of a clergyman.

It is inconceivable that amongst all the honours and glories which a girl expects from matrimony, the responsibility of worthily filling and elevating her position should be so little thought of. Ambition in this sense would be most useful to a woman.

Mrs. Vincent came about the beginning of March for a few days' visit to her young cousin, and was cheered and amused by her visit. She enjoyed the animated conversations, and intelligent interest in what went on in the world which distinguished both husband and wife, and the courteous kindness and consideration which Lord Mortimer

showed towards her were very pleasant to
the lonely woman.

She was delighted with the castle, and all
its quaint treasures and curiosities, and spent
many pleasant hours in examining the
various old books, prints, and engravings,
hangings, and china, which were gathered in
profusion within its walls.

There is something very charming in
roaming about an old English country house
and investigating its precincts; for many an
unpretentious-looking mansion contains
things which would adorn a palace, and too
often its owners are lamentably ignorant of
their valuable possessions, and keep the white
paint on their dark oak panellings, and look
at you in wonder when you suggest to them
that they are lucky to have such valuable
old Chelsea or Worcester, or admire their
Oriental vases.

There is a vast amount of ignorance amongst well-instructed people as to what is really beautiful ; and though schools of art are doing something to remove it, as long as people are so apathetic as to disregard the beauty or ugliness of their surroundings, so long will they hide away their china to put ormolu vases in its place, and prefer the ' cleanness ' and ' light ' appearance of white paint to the richness and colour of old oak.

One evening, during Mrs. Vincent's stay at Mortimer, Winnie, speaking of some neighbours whom she had been visiting that afternoon, said :

' What a quaint old house the Lisles live in, Rupert.   I was quite struck with it ; and that curious little square court inside the house is so uncommon.   It is provoking to think that the people who live in such a charming old place should be so " hum-drum "

—for no other word describes them—as the Lisles are.'

Lord Mortimer smiled as he answered :

'Yes, the Lisles are certainly not very interesting, but they are very good people in their way, and do a certain amount of good in their own village.'

'Still, with their means—for I suppose they are well off—it seems incredible that they should know and care so little about what is going on in the world. I think it is horrible for people to be so narrow-minded—don't you, Cousin Lucy ?'

'Tastes differ a good deal,' said Mrs. Vincent. 'I certainly don't like narrow-minded people ; but in this case, it seemed to me that the people we visited to-day were hardly that. They were more like what I should imagine a great many country squires' families were before railroad-days.'

'That is really the case,' remarked Lord Mortimer; 'the Lisles are complete old-world people, and such are very rare in these days.'

'A very good thing that they are rare,' was his wife's answer, 'for in the latter half of the nineteenth century they are quite out of place.'

'And yet,' said Mrs. Vincent, 'I think it is pleasant that some of those quiet people exist still. Variety in human nature is as pleasant as in other things, and there is nothing to me more striking in daily life than the wonderful difference of taste, ideas, and mode of life, between those who are, nominally at least, in the same rank of life.'

'As a variety you are quite welcome to like the Lisles,' said Winnie, laughing; 'but I am glad to believe they belong to a small species of the English race. To me the acme

of human misery would be to lead always a
monotonous country life, such as they lead
and seem to enjoy, devoid of all outward
interests and associations, and with so little
purpose in it.'

'It is fortunate, however, that every one is
not so decided in disliking country life as you
are, Winnie, seeing how many people have to
lead the dull lives you regard with such horror.
But it is always a puzzle to me whether it is
good or not to be satisfied with a narrow
sphere in life. I do not mean as regards
contentment, but rather that men and women
too, who might be capable of doing great
things, are yet willing to let their energies be
cramped, and their talents rendered useless.
by employing them only in a narrow sphere,
and so waste the powers entrusted to them.'

'Don't you think,' was Mrs. Vincent's
response to Lord Mortimer's remark, ' that

if people really fulfil the duties of their narrow sphere well, and do possess powers fitted for better things, that the opportunity for using their talents will come to them ?'

'Sometimes,' he answered, 'but not always. Too often, when a clever man leads a life without much scope for exertion, indolence steps in and makes him quite contented with small aims—in fact, takes from him that laudable ambition of exerting his own talents for the good of others which is one of the best incentives a man can have. In such a case a narrow sphere has been a positive misfortune to such a man, as in the bustle of ordinary life he must, to a certain extent, have mastered his indolence to go along with the tide.'

'But, Rupert,' exclaimed his wife, 'do you think that a really indolent man ever attains eminence in anything, whether his sphere is narrow, or world-wide ?'

'That is a fair question, and I am afraid indolence is a terrible bar to usefulness. But I was thinking less of a thoroughly in-dolent man than of one whose powers having proved sufficient for his daily duties without the least exertion on his part, so gets disin-clined to exert them at all.'

'In fact, one who lets his abilities rust !' exclaimed Winnie.

'Exactly; and to me there is no sadder spectacle.'

'I agree with you in a great measure,' said Mrs. Vincent, 'though I think a man who lets his faculties rust, in such a manner, can hardly have the real elements of usefulness, or any strong sense of duty. But wasted talents certainly are a sad spectacle, and when one thinks how many men have thrown away the possibilities of great careers from indolence or love of pleasure, it makes one mournful.'

'Another instance that no one can get on without ambition !' exclaimed Winnie. ' How could Shakespeare write, " Cromwell, I charge thee, fling away ambition "?—not that Cromwell took the advice though,' she added, laughing.

'Well,' replied her husband, 'I don't think it was wonderful that Shakespeare did not admire such ambitions as Wolsey's and Cromwell's—there is a wide difference between self-seeking ambition, and ambition which seeks the good of others.'

'Oh, certainly ; but while one admires the second sort the most, I think a little ambition on one's own account is very useful. Now, Rupert, you know you think so in your heart.'

'I own one does feel a good deal of sympathy with the inferior as well as the superior kind.'

'I think,' was Mrs. Vincent's comment, 'that as long as you admit both kinds of ambition to your sympathy, there is no fear of the first sort doing any harm.'

'No, Cousin Lucy, I am sure there is not ; and my own private belief is that people who are thoroughly unambitious are generally thoroughly useless too.'

'Well, Winnie, we will let you have the last word,' said Lord Mortimer, smiling.

'Which you can easily do, as you agree with it,' was her merry retort.

CHAPTER IX.

LORD MORTIMER'S DOUBTS.

' When a good woman
Is fitly mated she grows doubly good,
How good soe'er before.'
SHERIDAN KNOWLES.

ONE bright spring morning a few days afterwards, when **Mrs.** Vincent had returned **to** London, Lord Mortimer said at breakfast :

' Would **you** like to ride over **to** Royle to-day, **Winnie ?** I must go and see Sir Hugh about some county business, so I thought perhaps you might **come** as well.'

'I should like it very much ; it is such a fine morning, and I have been wanting to go to Royle for the last three weeks. What time shall you go ?'

'At twelve o'clock ; and coming back, if it is not too far for you, we might ride round by Beechington, and inspect the new farm there.'

'It will not be at all too far. I will be ready at twelve.'

And punctual to the appointed time Winnie came into the hall, where her husband joined her, and they were soon riding away in the direction of Royle.

Royle was about five miles from Mortimer, and fortunately the road leading to it was a good one for riding as well as driving. There was turf at the roadside, which is so delightful for a canter, and the turf was not broken up, as is often the case, by a succession of stone-heaps, or mysterious ridges, which prove so disappointing to an equestrian hoping for a good stretch of smooth ground.

So Winnie enjoyed her ride very much ; she was fond of riding, and was a good, though not a perfect, horsewoman. She could by no means ride 'anything,' and would probably have found Lilian Royle's ' Fury ' far beyond her powers of management ; but her pretty bay mare suited her perfectly, and she felt that exhilaration of spirits which a canter on a bright morning is sure to give.

They reached the lodge at Royle Abbey, and rode leisurely up the long avenue of oaks leading to the house.

' How lovely this avenue must be in summer !' exclaimed Winnie, as she glanced up towards the stately trees—leafless, it is true, but by their wide-spreading branches giving evidence of the delicious shade which might be found beneath them on a hot summer day.

'Yes, it is beautiful,' answered Lord Mortimer. 'The trees at Royle are splendid ; they are far better than any we have at home,' which was indeed the case ; and it is often curious to watch the difference in the growth of trees and shrubs in places, perhaps only a few miles apart, which in one case is often luxuriant, and in the other scanty.

Close to the hall-door the riders encountered Sir Hugh.

'Well, Mortimer, I am delighted to see you ; you're the very person I want a talk with. Lady Mortimer, my girls will be equally pleased to see you, for they were only saying this morning it was an age since they had met you.'

'It is a long time,' she said ; 'but the weather has been so bad, I have not been able to get over.'

Sir Hugh ushered her into the library,

where, as usual, Cicely was on her couch, and then carried off Lord Mortimer to his own sanctum for deliberation on some weighty business matters.

'This is a great pleasure,' said Cicely, as she welcomed her guest. 'I have so much to talk to you about; but first, I must congratulate you on your sister's engagement.'

'Oh, Kitty's—yes, thank you; we are all so glad that it is possible—thanks to Miss Haleswell's good offices. It will be a long engagement though, I am afraid.'

'I suppose it must be; still the time will pass—though in looking forward the years seem so much longer than in looking backward.'

'And it is very happy altogether; Captain Vernon is very nice in every way. I suppose you know him?'

'Yes, a little ; we have seen him when he has been with Miss Haleswell.'

'Miss Haleswell is like a fairy godmother !' exclaimed Winnie, 'who comes on the scene exactly at the moment when she is most needed. Kitty has been staying for a few days at Elm Court, and she writes such accounts of her kindness ; they seem to have made great friends.'

'I don't wonder at your sister liking Miss Haleswell, for she is so kind and good. We had a visit here from your brother too, some time ago ; he came down here with my brother for a night.'

'So he told me. He was delighted with the horse which he had just purchased from Sir Hugh.'

'Lilian was very enthusiastic about the horse,' said Cicely ; 'so I heard a great deal of its numerous good qualities, and hope that it will prove all that a horse should be. I am afraid to say anything else about it,' she added, laughing, 'as I am not very learned in horses.'

'Are you thinking of going away at all this summer?' asked Winnie, feeling that the time had come for finding out whether Lilian had any prospects of a season or not.

'No, I think not. I don't care much about moving, and my father does not like London for long; he will probably go up for a week or two with Lilian.'

'But is she not going up for the season? She would enjoy it so much.'

'I am sure she would; but I am afraid there is not much chance of her having a season. It would be too much of an undertaking for us to have a house, and we have no relations who would be able to chaperon her about to the proper number of balls and

parties; neither would Mary be able to take
her out regularly : so I don't think she has
any idea of going up for more than a few
days.'

'I am very sorry to hear it, for she is so
lovely, she would make quite a sensation.   I
hope you don't think me rude, but I can't
help telling you how much I admire her.'

'Indeed it is such a pleasure to me to hear
of Lilian being admired; she is so much
younger than Mary and I, that we look on
her almost more as a daughter than a sister,
so praise of her touches our motherly hearts.
There, Mary,' as her sister came in, 'Lady
Mortimer is delighting me with praises of
Lilian, which will charm you equally.'

'They will, certainly,' said Mary, her worn
face brightening at the mention of her darling.

'I have been telling your sister,' said Winnie, ' how sorry I am that Lilian is not going to London for the season, she would be so much admired.'

' It is very kind of you. I am very sorry also there is no chance of her going. She is so bright and happy, that she does not mind it in the least ; but I do wish she could have the enjoyment that a season gives ; indeed a London season is a kind of education in itself as well, I think.

' Yes,' said Cicely, ' it is never good for a girl to go into society only in her own county, especially when she has any looks ; she is sure to be rated too highly, and in London there are so many others more beautiful.'

' No !' exclaimed Winnie, ' Lilian need not fear comparison, in London or country either ; but I quite agree with you that it is a good thing to have the little rubs of London society. I enjoyed my two seasons as much as anybody: yet it was not all *couleur de rose;* and there are plenty of little vexations mixed up with the gaiety.'

' It is quite true,' said Mary Royle. ' I do not think a girl ever properly estimates her own value or finds her own level till she has seen how very little she is thought of in the crowd of London society.'

' So we are all agreed that, both for pleasure and profit, there is nothing so good as a London season,' said Winnie, laughing.

And just then they were interrupted by the entrance of Lilian herself, fresh from a ramble in the woods, and with her hands full of violets.

' Oh, I am so glad I am not late!' she exclaimed, after she had greeted Lady Mortimer. ' I have been to the mill, and had a long gossip with Mrs. Drayton, who was sadly, and very sorry for herself, so of course delighted to have a listener to her description of her ailments ; and then I came back through the plantations, and there were such quantities of violets that I could not resist stopping to get you some, Cicely.'

' Many thanks,' said her sister ; ' how lovely they are, and so delightfully sweet ! they will quite fill my large violet bowl.'

And for the next few minutes they all busied themselves in arranging the violets in water.

Like most invalids, Cicely had a passion for flowers ; and as this was well known, she was always kept well supplied with all kinds by her sisters and friends, and her room was generally filled with all sorts, from wild flowers to rare hothouse treasures.

When the Mortimers rode away from Royle that afternoon they passed out by another

road, and noticed how much timber had
been cut in that direction.

'What a shame!' was Winnie's comment,
'to cut down those beautiful old trees. I
wonder Sir Hugh can do it.'

'I am afraid,' answered her husband, 'that
Sir Hugh has no choice in the matter. It
is a question of money : for what with his
income never being large to begin with, and
his own open-handed way of living, combined
with the constant calls John Royle makes
on him, I suspect he is dreadfully hard
up.'

'How very sad ! Yes, I should not suppose Sir Hugh was of an economical turn of
mind.'

'The very reverse ; but it is a bad look-out
for those poor girls. I fear eventually they
will have very small fortunes.'

Winnie, thinking that now or never was

the time for her proposal about Lilian Royle, began :

'I suppose, then, that is the reason that Sir Hugh is not going to take Lilian to London for the season.'

'I don't think he could possibly afford it ; and even if he could, he does not love London.'

'We were talking about London, and her sisters regretted very much that she would not have a season.'

'Yes, I remember both of them had two or three seasons,' said Lord Mortimer.

'It made me think that I should like ——' began his wife rather nervously—'I mean—would you mind, Rupert, if Lilian came to us in May, and I took her out a little ?'

Winnie breathed more freely now that her proposal was fairly out, and turned her head to notice what effect her words had had on her husband.

He did not answer immediately, and after a pause, which Winnie feared did not augur well for her scheme, said :

‘ It is a very kind thought of yours, Winnie ; but I am afraid there are one or two serious objections to it.   However, we might consider it.’

This was so much more favourable than she had hoped, that Winnie took courage, and exclaimed :

‘ It seems so sad that any one so young and lovely as Lilian should not have a fair amount of enjoyment in her youth, more especially as there is so much trouble in her family.’

‘ That is very true ; but if she were less lovely I should be much more willing for you to take her out.   In fact, Winnie, it is a grave responsibility to take charge of a girl whose beauty is out of the common way.'

' Indeed, Rupert, I should be a very careful chaperon if I did take her out.'

' I don't doubt your good intentions, but you are not a hundred yet, and have not had a very long experience in the duties of a chaperon ? Besides, do you remember my old idea that your brother Geoffrey had taken a fancy to Lilian ? I should be very sorry to throw her in his way, and of course if she is with you he must see her constantly.'

' Oh yes, I remember ; but indeed, though you were right about Kitty, I do not see any danger for Geoffrey. Of course no one could see Lilian without admiring her ; but the other day he was speaking of having been down to Royle to buy a horse from Sir Hugh, and he did not talk in the least as if he had any special attraction there. He said the

Royles were very pleasant, and seemed struck with Cicely's cheerfulness; but there was nothing in that to make one fear he was in love with Lilian.'

Certainly Geoffrey de Valines had concealed his hopes and desires very skilfully.

'No, and there may be as you say no danger; but even supposing that objection is over-ruled, there is another, Lilian's brother. John Royle is not a man whom I will have in my house, and it is rather a difficult thing to prevent a brother's coming to see his sister.'

'Yes, that it certainly is. Is John Royle so very bad?'

'He is thoroughly bad, in every sense of the word; and I always expect he will end by doing something disgraceful which will finish his career in England at least. It was a great misfortune that poor Alan died; he was older than John, and as different from him as possible. Lady Royle never recovered his death ; indeed, she only lived a few months after the news reached her. But to return to Lilian : I have too much regard for the Royles to wish to stop anything which would give them all so much pleasure, as I am convinced your taking out Lilian would do, and yet I have a sort of feeling that it would be wiser not to take charge of her. She is wild too, and rather self-willed.'

'But not objectionably so, I should say ; and she is certainly not fast, in the sense in which girls generally are.'

'She is not, and a good deal of her apparent wildness may come from her having led such a free country life. Still, Winnie, I hesitate.'

'I would not for a moment wish to have her if you really disliked it.'

'It is not that I should dislike it, far from

it ; I should be glad to do a kindness to the
Royles, and to give pleasure to the girl herself, and it is very good-natured of you to be
willing to take her out.   But my doubt is,
whether it will be a prudent measure either
for her or for others.'

'I don't see how it could be an imprudent
measure for her.'

'She might wish to make some undesirable
marriage, and then we should be held respon-
sible.   And it is not as if she were a relation,
for we should really have no right to control
her.'

'But then again, she might make some
desirable acquaintance which would lead in
time to a really satisfactory marriage.'

'Ah, I see—your thoughts are busy at their
favourite employment of match-making.'

'Oh no, that is not match-making ; but I
should be very glad to give her an oppor-

tunity of seeing people, more especially after what you have told me as to her future prospects.'

'And it is when I think of them that I am inclined to say, you may ask her. After all, it is not an unnatural thing, and the Royles are amongst my oldest friends. Well, I will give a conditional consent now, Winnie, and in a week or two, if there is nothing to make me change, you may write and ask Lilian to stay with us for the season. Only I shall make it clear to Mary Royle that John must not expect to come to my house to see Lilian.'

'It is very good of you, Rupert, to consent,' said his wife, gratefully.

'Very good indeed of me, I think, as it will entail your going out perpetually; but I don't mind your doing so as a chaperon, so long as you don't become a "frisky matron" yourself, and that I should put a decided veto on.'

'Indeed, you may believe I have not the least inclination to become one.'

'No, I don't suspect you of the design, and your very willingness to undertake the chaperonage of a beauty is a proof that you don't mean to go out for your own amusement only. For if you were one of the present type of young married women, you would find a young lady an inconvenient appendage at a ball, though I believe that the fact of your being married would secure you the partners, and not Lilian.'

'Hardly, seeing what she is; but never fear, I think it is very unfair for the married women to take all the partners from the un-married girls. We have advantages enough, and it is hard on them to deprive them of the power of dancing, which, when the number of men is limited, the fact of the married women dancing certainly does. Those were my opinions as a girl, and, strange to say, I have not changed them since I married;' and she looked into her husband's face with a smile.

'Don't take too much credit to yourself, Winnie,' answered he; 'you were aware of my sentiments on the subject, and thought it wisest to give in—is not that a truer description of the case?'

'Certainly not,' laughed she, though knowing in her secret heart that there was a good deal of truth in his words; and they put their horses into a canter, and did not slacken speed till they reached Beechington, where they both dismounted and inspected the new farm there.

Winnie duly admired the new buildings, examined the various improvements, and inspected the dwelling-places ready for the herd of short-horns which were to take up their abode there. She was always ready to be interested in anything connected with her husband's estate, and greatly delighted the old farmer at Beechington by the attention she paid to his explanations. She even listened patiently to a long dissertation upon the harvest prospects, to which he treated Lord Mortimer, and which was certainly of the prosiest description. When they had gone the round of the farm buildings, he invited them to pay his wife a visit, and so Winnie was introduced to the worthy Mrs. Meadows, who, having had time since their arrival to adorn herself, appeared in all the glories of her Sunday black silk gown and best cap, and expressed herself as much delighted with her new abode.

'You see, my lady, it is so convenient and

nice ; the old house was nearly tumbling down. Not but what I was sorry to leave the old place, for I had gone there when I was married, five-and-thirty years ago, my lady, come Michaelmas, and had seven children there ; four lie in the churchyard, my lady, and my daughter's married, and one of my sons is a clerk in London, so we've only Jack at home, and he helps his father. But, dear me, and won't you take some refreshment, my lady, after your long ride ?'

'No, thank you, Mrs. Meadows ; indeed it is getting late, and I think we must be going.'

'Well, I'm sure I'm most honoured to have had a visit from your ladyship, and no one thinks more of my lord and his family than I do; my father lived on the estate all his life, and Meadows and his father and grandfather have had this Beechington farm for seventy years and more.'

'And I am sure Lord Mortimer is very glad to have such good tenants,' said Winnie, who fortunately remembered to have heard her husband praise old Meadows.

Highly pleased at the compliment, Mrs. Meadows stood smiling and curtseying at the door till they had ridden out of sight, and turned back into the house full of praises of the young countess. As the Mortimers dismounted at home, one of the servants said :

'Mr. Percival is here, my lord ; he came by the four o'clock train. He's in the library.'

'Winnie, do you hear?' exclaimed her husband; 'Tom's here—an unexpected visitor, for I thought he was so busy just now in London.'

CHAPTER X.

THE CHESTON ELECTION.

'Let Whig and Tory stir their blood,
There must be stormy weather;
But for some true result of good
All parties work together.'

TENNYSON.

LORD MORTIMER went at once to the library, and his wife followed him, curious to hear what had brought Tom Percival down from London so suddenly.

'Well, Tom !' exclaimed his cousin, as he entered ; 'I'm delighted to see you, but it was quite a surprise to hear of your arrival.'

'I should think so,' answered Tom; 'and only urgent business would have brought me just now. I heard this morning that old Bridgburn is dead.'

'Bridgburn dead! you don't say so? I did not know he was ill!'

'Neither was he; it was quite sudden: he had a seizure yesterday afternoon, and died in the evening. I heard it this morning at the Carlton, and thought I had better run down and talk over my prospects with you.'

'I am very glad you did. Well, of course when the funeral is over, you will be brought forward as the Conservative candidate, and then you must canvass as hard as you can. I hope you have a fair chance of success, but you'll have a troublesome opponent if, as I expect, the Liberals start Daniels, the retired brewer, against you.'

'I should like a good fight, and am sanguine about success. Cheston has always been true blue, and it always must be.'

'I hope it will, but there is a good deal more of the Radical element in Cheston than there was.'

'Oh, I know that; and I expect it will be a close contest. Winnie, I hope you are prepared to help me in canvassing?'

'I shall be delighted to do anything I can; and will call on all the old worthies in Cheston, if that will be any good.'

'That will be a help. Well, let us consider time. Easter is late, and I should think the writ will be out, and the election take place a fortnight before Easter; so we have not got too much time.'

'No, indeed,' answered Lord Mortimer; 'if you can stay over to-morrow, Tom, you might see Cartwright and Sharpe.'

'Yes, but that I can't manage; I must go back after dinner to-night. There's a train about ten, and I must be at my work to-morrow, more especially as I shall want nearly three weeks' holiday.'

The remainder of Tom's Percival's flying visit was spent in animated discussion respecting his chances of success, his probable supporters, and the number of doubtful voters who might be induced to vote for him.'

'I am almost sorry,' remarked Winnie, 'that the old days of elections are gone by; there is not much excitement in these times of the ballot.'

'There certainly was plenty of that, not to mention a great amount of rowdyism, under the old system,' said her husband. 'I remember, when I sat for Cheston, there was a tremendous row at one election. I do not like secret **voting, but so** far as the present system prevents a commotion, it is **a** good thing; though I'm afraid I'm no believer **in the** purity **of** elections even **under the ballot.'**

'On the contrary,' said Tom, laughing, 'it gives an avaricious voter a chance of being bribed **by** both sides with perfect impunity, as no one can tell which way he votes at the **last.** However, as far as regards **myself, I'm** not going to try bribery and **corruption, and I** only hope **my** kind supporters won't **do** it for me. Don't **you** remember, Mortimer, when Sewell was **un**seated for Sandby, through the **kind officiousness** of his **agents?** It was **quite a case of** " Defend **me** from **my** friends." '

'Yes,' said **Lord** Mortimer ; 'and till you can make the average English elector regard his vote as something else besides a marketable commodity, you will never do away with bribery. However great the outcry for extension of the franchise may be, I don't believe one half of the men who have it already value their votes in the least. They do not consider the stake they have in the country, or the power of a vote, and only desire the franchise as a means of gaining some advantage, monetary or otherwise, at an election.'

' I wish there were some means of remedying it,' said Tom; ' perhaps, in time, education may do something.'

' It may. I hope it will;' and the announcement that the carriage was waiting obliged Tom to hurry away to catch his train.

' I cannot make out,' said Winnie, ' why men who have got votes value them so little,

and yet make such an outcry for the extension of the franchise.'

' I think that outcry,' replied her husband,
' proceeds from a sort of vague notion that
household suffrage would enable them to
elect members from their own class, who
would, as they think, better the condition of
the working man. Most certainly those
means will never better the working man
while their present ignorance of what would
help them remains. As regards the value of
their vote, they don't appreciate it because,
as a rule, I fear they have no higher aims
than getting more wages for less work, which
generally ends in their spending more in
drink.'

' Oh, how sad it is ! one does so wish there
was some means of getting better ideas into
their heads.'

' It will be a long time before that is done.

I am sure one means of helping them is to secure them good houses fit for human habitation, which too many of the poorest dwelling-houses are not.'

' And your bill will help that ?'

' I hope so ; good houses would help them to self-respect, which would lead to habits of providence and foresight. Another very important thing would be, if it were possible, to circulate a higher stamp of newspaper amongst the working classes, one which would give them enlarged ideas as to their real needs and opportunities. A poor man puts immense faith in what he calls " my paper," and it is very difficult to shake his confidence in what it tells him ; and when one considers how trashy and mischievous too many of the newspapers they get are, one feels sorry that they do not possess the means of getting better information.'

'But there are good penny papers.'

'Oh, certainly; but the poor man's newspaper is generally a weekly penny one, full of horrors to satisfy the public taste for such things. If we can get more reading-rooms and coffee-rooms opened for the working man, in them at least he will find better newspapers, and books too, suited to him, and likely to interest him. The poor man wants amusement and relaxation quite as much as the rich man—indeed more, for he cannot get any quiet place at home. But I am afraid, Winnie, these are utopian ideas, very unlikely to be realised, at least in our times.'

'Still, people are beginning to pay more attention to these things.'

'Yes, and that of itself is an improvement; all things must be gradual which produce changes, if they are to do real good. If only every landlord were compelled to keep the houses he owns in proper repair, a great step would be gained, and the larger land-lords might probably be induced to do so; but then there arises the difficulty of the very small proprietors, who are often posi-tively unable to spend any of their small rents on repairs. I always pity these small landlords, who are supposed "to have money" because they own two or three tumbledown cottages, but who are generally poorer than the ordinary labourer. The best thing that can happen is for their tenements to be bought up by the larger landlords, and yet they are often unwilling to sell them. How-ever, I have bought up most of them round about here.'

'And the small proprietors of land are just as badly off,' continued Winnie. 'What would become of the country if the extreme

Radicals were to realise their ideas on the division of lands ?'

' I cannot think the system of peasant proprietors would answer in England ; if it were adopted it would probably only last a few years, and then the industrious man would be able to buy up his idle neighbour's holding, while the idle man would probably answer, if he was asked what he wished to be done, as I believe a man in similar circumstances once did answer : " Why, then I'd be all for dividing again." Besides, in England, before the system of small holdings could be adopted, the land would have to be taken from its present owners, and such an injustice would hardly be possible without a revolution, which I hope England will be long spared.'

In three or four days, Tom Percival came down from London and began his canvassing

in good earnest, while Winnie paid any
number of visits in Cheston ; and many
were their stories of the various experiences
they met with, whenever Tom had a
spare half-hour in which to discuss his pro-
ceedings.

Winnie was paying a visit one day to Mrs.
Boultbee, the lady who had owned the
cameos at the Cheston ball. Now Mrs.
Boultbee being a widow, with no children,
was not of course likely to possess any influence as regarded votes ; and Winnie showed
great impartiality in her visits, to prevent
any idea of undue influence from Mortimer
being suggested.

She felt convinced that she should hear a
great deal of information, more or less interesting, about the chances of the election
from Mrs. Boultbee, who was one of those
people who possess the power of collecting

all kinds of gossip ; nor was she disappointed.

'Well, Lady Mortimer, I am delighted to see you ; and I hope you are as anxious for Mr. Percival's success as I am.'

'I think I may own to being very anxious. Now, Mrs. Boultbee, you always know all that is going on in Cheston, do tell me what is said of his chances of success.'

Highly pleased to be considered an authority, Mrs. Boultbee began :

'Oh, I have every hope ; but now, to tell you the truth, that Daniels is a horrid bad candidate to fight against. You see, having been a brewer, he has got such a hold over the townspeople ; and I am afraid the publicans will all go with him, for they say he takes a share in the brewery still. Of course I am not speaking of Mr. Price of the Red Lion, who's a most respectable man, and has always voted for my lord's candidate.'

'Oh, but pray remember that Lord Mortimer does not wish to influence any of his tenants.'

'Of course not—of course not—quite right too,' said Mrs. Boultbee, with a series of knowing little nods. 'I know all about that, Lady Mortimer; it was only a slip, and did not matter to you; and of course every tenant of Lord Mortimer's ought to be much obliged to him for letting them have freedom of choice, and the only way they can show their gratitude is by voting for Mr. Percival. No influence in that, Lady Mortimer,' said Mrs. Boultbee, with a hearty laugh. 'But I was telling you about Daniels : he is a nasty sort of Radical Dissenter, and is always stirring up the people; and his wife, too, is such a woman—nothing but an innkeeper's daughter, Lady Mortimer, if you'll believe me, and so stuck up ! She's spending money pretty fast, I can assure you ; but however, her husband's not in yet: still I don't like his having bought all those houses.'

'What houses ?' asked Lady Mortimer.

' Most of those in Castle Street ; he did not buy them in his own name either, but he's known as the owner now, and I hear he has given the occupants to understand that if they don't support him they will have notice to quit. But now, Lady Mortimer, that must be an idle threat ; I thought the voting was all secret now. I am sure there's been fuss enough about the Ballot Act.'

' It is supposed to be secret, certainly. But what a horrid thing to do ! I call it intimidation ; but I dare say the poor men will vote for him, for fear he should turn them out:

and of course if he works on the voters by threats, it is a bad look-out.'

' He'll only get the low class of voters by those means,' said Mrs. Boultbee, consolingly, ' and there are many respectable people in Cheston to counterbalance them. Dear me, how well I recollect the first time your husband was elected for Cheston, Lady Mortimer! What a to-do there was, to be sure; what flags and banners, and such a procession, and he and all his supporters, my poor husband amongst them, riding through the town; and then the hurrahing! They may say what they like, but an election was a fine sight in those days, and pleased everybody.'

' Well, good-bye Mrs. Boultbee. I'm afraid we shall have a very close run.'

' Let us hope for the best. I shall do anything in my small way to aid Mr. Percival that I can. Such a merry pleasant young man he is! He ran in here last evening, and asked me to give him a cup of tea. I said, "Mr. Percival, I'm only too pleased, but I hope you'll take a glass of wine instead—it will do you more good—or a brandy and soda now?" But he wouldn't be persuaded to have that; he said he knew my tea of old, and should prefer it. So I gave him a good cup, indeed he had two; in fact I may say I'm very particular about having good tea. Now, Lady Mortimer, will you stay and honour me by taking a cup?'

'Indeed, I should like it, but I must really hurry away; I'm late as it is.'

The next day Winnie paid a visit to the old lady who, at the Cheston Ball, had been so anxious to have the Duchess of Newport pointed out to her. She was a certain old Miss Quatermaine who kept house for her brother, head clerk in **Sherby's bank.** Lady Mortimer's visit put her into a great flutter of delight, and she came into the little stiff prim parlour, into which her guest had been ushered, with an amusing mixture of respect and satisfaction.

' Why to be sure, how careless of Eliza ! she never lighted the fire in here. Won't you step into the other room, my lady ? it is so cold here.'

Be it known that, in spite of Miss Quatermaine's lamentations over Eliza's neglect, she was well aware of the fact that there was no fire in the best parlour ; indeed there never was one, excepting on the rare occasions when Miss Quatermaine gave a tea-party, a circumstance which the cold and stuffiness of the room had made Lady Mortimer suspicious of; and she was much relieved when the old lady, contented with having shown that she had a best parlour, led her into a cosy sitting-room with a good fire.

'Poor Mr. Bridgburn's death quite unexpected I hear,' began Miss Quatermaine, after various civilities had passed.

'Yes, it seems to have been quite sudden.'

'Poor old gentleman! he was much respected, and his widow will enjoy a very comfortable fortune, so she's reason to revere his memory. But Mr. Percival's election quite cheers us up, after hearing of Mr. Bridgburn's death.'

'I hope it will be his election, and that he will succeed in winning the day.'

'Indeed I hope so, my lady; surely there can be no doubt, such a nice young gentleman as he is. My brother has a high opinion of him; I am thankful to say, my lady, my brother is a good old Conservative, quite opposed to these new-fangled ways. I have been reading Mr. Percival's speech in the *Herald*, and I see he says " he has long had the ambition to represent Cheston in Parliament ;" quite a compliment to our poor little town, my lady, and so prettily put l'

' I think Cheston is a very flourishing town, Miss Quatermaine, and there seem some good shops in it.'

' Does your ladyship think so ? Well, now, I am pleased to hear it ; and certainly Lily-white the draper is a very respectable fair-dealing tradesman, and so is Clark the stationer. But we are unfortunate in our butchers, my lady ; they are all dissenters.'

Winnie could not help smiling at the old lady's remarks, who further went on : ' How-ever, I must say it is a comfort they are all alike in that respect, for I always think how unfortunate it would be if the bad one was a church-going man ; we should feel ourselves bound to employ him. But it is so unpleasant not to get good meat !'

'Very unpleasant indeed,' answered Winnie, much amused.

'And I am so glad you like Cheston,' pursued Miss Quatermaine, on whom a word of praise of her native town was never thrown away ; ' it certainly is superior to most country towns, and we have many resident gentry : our good vicar of course at the head, then his curates—one of them, Mr. Young, is such a good young man ; only he is so shy, he's almost afraid of the sound of his own voice ; and then Mr. and Mrs. Sherby at the bank, and two lawyers, and three doctors, and Mrs. Boultbee, and two clergymen's widows, and a retired lawyer—oh, and many more I assure you, my lady ; not to mention that horrid Mr. Daniels, whom I don't like to name in your ladyship's presence.'

'You need not mind that,' answered Lady Mortimer, laughing, 'for I hear his name perpetually.'

'Well, of course since he's presumed to oppose Mr. Percival, his name is a good deal heard. Such a want of proper respect to Lord Mortimer's family ! His mother was a very good woman, too ; I am thankful she's not lived to see the day when her son went against a Percival.'

Certainly Miss Quatermaine was an ardent partisan of Tom Percival's, and Winnie was glad to think she had heard of one man likely to vote for him, in the old lady's brother, for she was getting rather doleful as to the prospects of success.

One of Tom Percival's own most satisfactory visits was paid to the house of Mr. Rawlings, the seedsman ; it was literally to the house, as Mr. Rawlings was not at home.

But the house was not unoccupied, for Mrs. Rawlings, who was in every respect her husband's better half, was at home, and received Mr. Percival in her parlour. She was a tall rather good-looking woman, with red cheeks and black ringlets, and was smartly dressed.

Now her husband was believed to incline in politics to the Liberal side, and so Tom had been anxious for a conversation with him. But he knew Rawlings by sight as a small meek man ; and when he saw his buxom spouse, he began to think that he might do as well by a conversation with her, as he felt an inward conviction that she ruled her lord and master, and not he her.

Tom began, however : ' I am sorry, Mrs. Rawlings, not to see your husband. I wanted to have had a talk with him about politics.' -

' Oh, sir ! the election, I suppose; no doubt

you are very busy. Well, of course it is not for me to say which way Rawlings will vote, but Mr. Daniels is a very good customer, and he would not wish to offend him.'

' Of course not. Why, Mrs. Rawlings, what an extremely pretty little girl you've got !' taking the child on his knee, and holding out his watch to it. ' Extremely pretty, and yet, Mrs. Rawlings'—and he fixed his eyes on that lady with an admiring glance—' I do not think she will ever equal her mother.'

' La, now ! Mr. Percival, you're too polite !' exclaimed Mrs. Rawlings, with a coquettish simper. ' Ah, I know what you London gentlemen are for paying compliments ! I know London pretty well myself, having stayed with my aunt, who keeps a most superior lodging-house for gentlemen in John of Groat's Lane, Islington. I dare say you know it, sir.'

'No, I hardly think I do,' said Tom, reflecting; 'but then, you see, my work is quite in the opposite direction. My chambers in the Temple are a long way from Islington, I am sorry to say.'

'Yes, of course,' replied Mrs. Rawlings, with an air of perfect acquaintance with London, though in reality she had not the vaguest idea where the Temple was. 'Well, Mr. Percival, if you are ever wanting comfortable apartments in Islington, I am sure my aunt would be happy to accommodate you. Many nice gentlemen she's had for lodgers, I can tell you, sir; so pleasant spoken and polite as they were;' and Mrs. Rawlings gave a sigh which was intended to convey to Tom the knowledge that the gentlemen in question had been specially attentive to her.

So his answer gave her satisfaction. ' I am

sure, Mrs. Rawlings, they could not be otherwise to you,' he said gallantly.

She smiled and simpered, and said in a would-be sad tone :

'Ah well, I like to remember old times, I often tell Rawlings there was many a one envied him when I married him.'

'Indeed, Mrs. Rawlings, your husband is a fortunate man ; I wish I could have seen him to tell him so. However, I have been the gainer in making your acquaintance.'

And with a profound bow and pressure of her hand, Tom took his departure, hoping that, in spite of the absence of the seedsman, he had done something towards securing his vote. And as Mrs. Rawlings watched him down the street, she said to herself :

'He's a real gentleman, he is ; and very

much he admired me, poor young man ! So
different from that Daniels; when he came
yesterday, he says, so short, " Is Rawlings
in ?" and when I said " No, sir," he only
said, " Tell him I called to see him," and
was off again without so much as a " good-
day." Well, I am determined of one thing :
I don't care nothing for what Rawlings says
about that Daniels being a good customer ; he
shall give his vote to that nice young gentleman, Mr. Percival, as sure as my name is
Selina Jane.'

And it may be mentioned that Mrs.
Rawlings was as good as her word, and that,
sheltered by the secrecy of the ballot, as
he hoped, from the fear of Mr. Daniels'
displeasure, the seedsman duly recorded his
vote for Tom Percival.

Tom's next visit was to an eccentric old
man named Stedman, usually credited with

possessing a good sum of money, and with being a miser. Certainly his appearance was wretched and dirty enough, as Tom was ushered into the room he was sitting in, by an ill-favoured old woman. Neither was his greeting propitious. 'So you've come after my vote?' he snarled.

'Not unless you choose to give it me,' returned Tom, coolly. 'I have come to tell you what my opinions are, and then you'll be able to decide for yourself whether you approve of them.'

'And what are they?' growled old Stedman, a little less fiercely.

'They are Conservative,' answered Tom, with a quick glance round the apartment, 'and I shall always support measures calculated to preserve order and quietness in the country, and while neglecting no means to improve the condition of all classes, to secure to every man the lawful enjoyment of his own possessions——'

Apparently this was a line of argument that Mr. Stedman approved of, for he gave a sort of grunt of approval, and said :

'Every man has a right to keep his own, but you'll never improve those who spend all their money before they have it.

'I hope in time they will learn greater providence, and save a little.'

'Not they; there aren't many like me, I've taken good care not to waste my hard-earned savings,' with a chuckle ; 'not but what I've got very little. I am a poor man,' he continued, and then added suddenly—'I'll take five pounds for it,' and cunningly glanced up at Tom.

'No, Mr. Stedman,' said he, rising ; 'you've mistaken me. I did not come to buy your vote, only to let you have an opportunity of knowing my side of the question. So if you have nothing further to ask me, I won't trouble you any longer.'

With an amazed air, the old man gazed at him. 'I won't peach on you,' he said with a grin, as he looked into Tom's face, 'and you'll want every vote you can get. It is not such a high price either; I got ten pounds one election.'

'Please understand that I don't want to get into Parliament by bribery,' answered Tom, warmly. 'It is not that I care what expenses come to, so long as they are fair and honest ones, but I don't call buying votes either; so you've got the wrong man for that, Mr. Stedman. Good-day;' and Tom took his departure, leaving the old man astonished.

'He'll never get in,' said the miser to himself, 'if he's not a little more ready with his money. What are they come to, to grudge five pounds for a vote! why, Daniels could not expect to get mine for less. And if I don't get fair pay, I won't vote at all;' with which the old wretch consoled himself, while Tom hurried away, very indignant at being asked for a bribe.

As, however, old Stedman did appear at the voting-place, we may suspect that Mr. Daniels or his agents were not so scrupulous as Tom.

Very hard Tom worked, and very anxious were the conferences which he held with his committee and supporters, and very eager the debates at Mortimer, when he had a few spare minutes to discuss progress with Lord Mortimer and Winnie.

Winnie was much amused at the account of Mrs. Rawlings, and very indignant at old Stedman's behaviour :

'Horrid old man!' she exclaimed; 'and that's an enlightened English elector!'

'Not enlightened, exactly,' said her husband, laughing; 'old Stedman's eccentricities belong to the dark ages, I think. The idea of his asking directly what Tom would give for his vote is worthy of *Punch.*

'Really,' said Tom, 'an election is a wonderful thing for showing people's characters. One sees a very ugly side of human nature when one is canvassing; but then there is a good deal of interest and kind feeling as well. And in the working men's hall I had a fairly intelligent audience, though very few had votes. They were delighted when I told them that, as far as

I was personally concerned, I wished they all had votes, for I was convinced if they had, that they would give them to me. And by their cheers, I believe theywould. Well, the day after to-morrow is the election; and I shall be most thankful when it is over. I only hope it may give me the right to stick M.P. after my name.'

Winnie was in a state of intense excitement on the day fixed for the polling. 'Really, Rupert,' she exclaimed to her husband, 'I'm quite glad you're not in the House of Commons now, for what I should do if you had a contested election I don't know. I am anxious enough as it is, but that would be ten thousand times worse.'

'You would have to take example by Mrs. Beauchamp,' answered her husband, 'who, when Beauchamp was elected, stayed in London all the time, and said how thankful she was not to be at their own place; it would have bored her so to be obliged to seem to care whether he got in or not.'

'Horrible woman!' cried Winnie; 'no, indeed I should never have a happy moment till I knew you had succeeded.'

'As perhaps I might have failed, Winnie, I am glad you are spared the anxiety; however, I quite agree with you that an election is an exciting business, and that I shall be very glad when the result of this one is known. I wonder whether the poll will be declared to-night?'

This question was answered about ten that evening, when a note was brought to Lord Mortimer, on which was hastily scrawled the result of the poll :

'PERCIVAL . . . 653

DANIELS . . . 610

'All right !

'T. P., M.P.'

Winnie gave an exclamation of delight as her husband read out the numbers.

'Oh, I am so glad! it is capital, and a better majority than Tom hoped for at the best.'

'Yes, it is. Well, I am rejoiced at it ; for I felt very doubtful as to the result. I hope he will soon be back to receive our congratulations.'

And when the hero of the day arrived, an hour later, he certainly received the warmest possible congratulations from his cousins.

Tom was indeed much pleased at his election, though he declared he felt he should be a sleeping member of the House for a long time, after the amount of fatigue and speechifying he had undergone during the last three weeks.

END OF VOL. I.

BILLING AND SONS, PRINTERS, GUILDFORD, SURREY.

www.ingramcontent.com/pod-product-compliance
Lightning Source LLC
Chambersburg PA
CBHW030807020726
47499CB00006B/1804